"SWEET DEATH, KIND DEATH
is another splendid whodunit filled with all the
good things we've come to expect from Ms. Cross:
intelligence, urbanity, and wonderful, wry
humor. . . .Amanda Cross has done it again."
Susan Isaacs
Author of *Almost Paradise*

"AMANDA CROSS
mysteries are the kind one can recommend
wholeheartedly, not only to fans of the genre but
to people who never usually read mysteries at
all."
Publishers Weekly

"KATE FANSLER
is the treasure at the center of all Cross's cerebral
puzzles, intelligent, self-doubting, one of those
rare people who quote scores of writers
unself-consciously and to the point."
Newsweek

SWEET DEATH, KIND DEATH
AMANDA CROSS
A Kate Fansler Mystery

SWEET DEATH, KIND DEATH

Amanda Cross

BALLANTINE BOOKS • NEW YORK

Library of Congress Catalog Card Number: 84-1469

ISBN 0-345-31177-9

This edition published by arrangement with E.P. Dutton, Inc.

Manufactured in the United States of America

First Ballantine Books Edition: March 1985

Why do I think of Death
As a friend?
It is because he is a scatterer,
He scatters the human frame
The nerviness and the great pain,
Throws it on the fresh fresh air
And now it is nowhere.
Only sweet death does this,
Sweet Death, kind Death,
Of all the gods you are best.

STEVIE SMITH

Chapter 1

This is the simplest of all thoughts, that Death must come
when we call, although he is a god.
STEVIE SMITH

> For a life of the writer and teacher Patrice Umphelby, we would appreciate hearing from anyone who has letters from her or personal knowledge of her.

*T*he New York City memorial service for Patrice Umphelby (for she had, of course, had a funeral service at Clare College many months earlier), was attended by Kate Fansler and several hundred other people, all of whom found it uniquely moving. Services for the dead may be deeply sad, and they are rarely uplifting. Patrice's service was run as a Quaker funeral, with those who wished to testify to their experience of the dead woman rising to do so. In Kate's experience, and she was, she felt, hardly alone in this, such an unstructured format was to be dreaded: it empowered the loquacious and silenced those with profound memories or feelings. In this case, however, her fears were unjustified. Each account, from men who had known Patrice

1

in her youth and since, from women whom she had encouraged in her middle age, testified to her spirit, her radiance, her generosity, above all, to the attention she seemed able to offer those to whom she spoke. Kate had not known Patrice Umphelby, but she had heard, before Patrice's death and after it, such vibrant recollections of her that she had gone to the memorial service out of a kind of necessity to mark the passing of a woman uniquely courageous. Many at the service were silent, yet even that silence, it seemed to Kate, spoke of loss and of the promised persistence of memory. Since the memorial service, Patrice Umphelby had hovered behind Kate's thoughts; her name was often mentioned, her spirit invoked. And then, suddenly, she was recalled to Kate's attention, and in a particularly compelling way.

Kate had not seen the announcement in the *New York Times Book Review* and other journals of the proposed biography of Patrice. She first heard there was to be a biography of the dead woman when she, Kate, was at home with the flu, lying in bed and feeling that profound indifference to the continuation of the world which the flu notoriously induces. Her awareness that the world, in this nuclear age of weaponry, might not in any case continue did not mitigate the profundity of her indifference. What was clear to the merest intelligence was that the viruses or bacteria (or whatever neologistic nomenclature attached itself to the beastly organisms that thrived upon the human body when in a state of immunity supression) had strengthened themselves in their recent battles against modern medicine and would, with the fortune that had ever accompanied their species, survive the demolition of all other sentient life.

Why, in this event, she was determined to read her mail she found it impossible to explain. Reed Amhearst, her husband, cooperated with this, to him, lunatic intention to the extent of opening the envelopes for her and piling the letters within reach. The letter from the two men said that they were writing Patrice's biography, and would like to speak to Kate about her. Did Kate remember meeting with Patrice in a fog-bound airport some years ago and talking about God?

Kate lay back on the pillows and closed her eyes. So one waits for a film just loaded into the projector to unwind and focus itself. No, she thought, the phenomenon of middle-aged memory was more like a sudden picture flashed before the mind as magic lanterns used to be flashed; no doubt these days, if magic lanterns existed at all, they were called audio-visual aids. In middle age, Kate found, memory returned unsummoned, or summoned by the merest word, smell, or sound, and blazed for a moment in the brain. If one was, like Kate, an evader of memories, a loather of tales from the past, these flashes were allowed to disappear. (Much later, thinking back on this fluish moment when Patrice's name had been recalled to her, Kate would realize that this disdain for memory was something she and Patrice, with a certain wild eccentricity, shared.)

Patrice (her biographers had written) had, of course, been christened Patricia, but had since girlhood delighted in the French form of Patrick, even as George, the young woman friend of Nancy Drew, had delighted in the name of George. Reed, appearing at that moment with a glass of orange juice, was asked if he remembered that Nancy Drew, to whom he had once compared Kate—very unkindly she had thought at the time—had a female friend named George? Reed's disdain for this question equaled in vehemence Kate's disdain for the orange juice. Flu is one of the hazards of marriage infrequently mentioned in discussions of the burgeoning divorce rate.

It came back to Kate only now in a fluish haze that the men were right: she and Patrice had met once, years earlier, in a fog-bound airport in Scotland, where, forced to await the dissipation of the fog, they had been offered neither sustenance nor facilities of a

3

more than primitive order. (Kate, as was widely known among her friends, could stand anything if provided with drink and adequate plumbing.) Kate and Patrice, collapsed near one another on those unyielding seats beloved of airports, had mutually sighed. Kate had then produced from her carry-on luggage a flask containing Laphroaig (this was long before that delectable malt beverage became a stylish item in the United States) and had offered Patrice, name as yet unknown, a slug. They had moved then, by obvious stages, from malt to God, and questions about his existence. The subject had, Kate was certain, been introduced by Patrice; it was not one Kate was likely to bring up at anytime, least of all when in fog-bound airports. Kate had, on being questioned, declared, in a sentence she had formulated in her early twenties and never found any reason for altering, that she supposed belief in God was a comfort to those who could not contemplate the unfairness of life without such melioration. And then, Kate remembered, (it must be assumed that she had, by now, consumed more than one slug of Laphroaig) she had quoted Mrs. Ramsay from Woolf's *To the Lighthouse*.

" 'What had brought her to say that: "we are in the hands of the Lord"? . . . How could any Lord have made this world? she asked. With her mind she had always seized the fact that there is no reason, order, justice: but suffering, death, the poor. There was no treachery too base for the world to commit; she knew that. No happiness lasted; she knew that.' "

"Do you always quote Virginia Woolf?" Patrice had asked.

"Quoting, like smoking," Kate had answered, "is a dirty habit to which I am devoted. But then," she had added, as she almost never did to chance acquaintances met traveling, "I am a professor of English literature: it is an occupational hazard."

"Ah," Patrice had said, "I too am a professor,

though not of literature, and I do not quote, at least not when talking. But you are right: there is no God."

The two men writing the biography of Patrice Umphelby, when Kate, in the fullness of time and the subsiding of her flu, met them, turned out to be named Archer and Herbert, and to bring to this interview, as they had no doubt brought to many others, a combination of charm and seriousness that was irresistible, at least to Kate. They managed to convey, with on Archer's part, delicate flattery, on Herbert's part, puzzled earnestness, that in Kate they had found a treasure. Kate, who had long since decided on the general rule that first impressions can never be trusted, settled back in contemplation of new friends and the giddy pleasure of abandoning general rules.

The restaurant itself contributed to their mood of pleased discovery. Kate, who had often accused herself of conducting her entire social life, and that part of her professional life not spent in class and committee rooms, across a restaurant table, had become a connoisseur of restaurants—not of the food, but of the ambience: the space between tables, the attention of waiters, a promptness of service not inspired by a desire to get the table for someone else, and a women's room that was suitable, at best, to a youth hostel. Beyond that, as far as Kate was concerned, Mimi Sheraton might rant and rave, but as long as they did not deep fry soft-shelled crabs or put a sauce on everything, Kate was undemanding. She ate out, after all, to talk. Reed would have said, had he not been so nice, that she lived to talk.

This restaurant, which was Chinese, promised, like her lunch companions, to meet Kate's standard of sociability.

"But Patrice," Kate asked Archer and Herbert, "was she the sort to care for elegant restaurants, even of an Asiatic order? She struck me as eccentric, at least to the extent that an older woman more devoted to comfort than elegance or maintaining the illusion of

5

youth can be called eccentric in our society. Would she not have rather, for example, lapped yogurt out of a container and taken a brisk walk?''

"Oh, dear yes," Archer said. "She was madly eccentric by any normal womanly standards, and wholly delightful, which is, my dear, a rare combination. I mean most women who have abandoned fashion and elegance, which tends to mean, let's face it, flat shoes and grubby nails—well, one does so often feel when talking to them that one should be ready to die on the barricades for whatever it is they're being so earnest about, and one doesn't often feel barricadish, one feels like lunching delightfully, like this.''

Herbert, the serious one, looked troubled. Kate surmised his role in the partnership to be that of getting the nose to the grindstone, the trousers to the desk chair, the footnotes in place, the sources tracked down. He was clearly as essential to Archer as Archer to him. Archer it was who charmed the friends and relations of Patrice, enticing from them the memories and stories essential to any biography, enticing them, first of all, into meeting him. No doubt, alone, Archer would have spent his days in frivolity, Herbert in dullness, equally unproductive.

Yet Herbert was troubled because Archer seemed to be rescuing Patrice from a stereotype by condemning other women to it; seemed, furthermore, to be flattering Kate beyond the degree a woman of her intelligence might expect to be flattered. Kate honored Herbert for this, but knew too that Herbert could not see beyond Archer's nonsense to the kindness, the perceptiveness, which hovered beneath it. Archer, Kate guessed, was never unkind; he responded to intimate signals lost upon Herbert and most other people; for this reason, Archer was universally loved. Yet he needed Herbert, loving life so much, since without Herbert, Archer would not have stopped living long enough to record life's passing. Together, these two would perpetrate a biography. Kate, before she had finished her lunch, had

6

fallen in love with both of them. And this marked what was unusual in Kate, what Archer had recognized. Most people fell in love only with Archer.

As, it appeared, Patrice had done.

"How," Kate asked, as inevitably she had to, "do you two come to be writing Patrice's biography? Why two men, and why a biography at all? All I know about Patrice really, you see, is that she was a professor, widely known and widely loved, and that she did not believe in God."

"An astonishing number of people wanted to write Patrice's biography—you'd be quite nonplused, my dear. Her children, who are her heirs, tried to follow her wishes, or what they presumed would be her wishes under the circumstances, and opened her papers to anyone who asked. My dear, the crowds, the noise, the people, as Ernest Thesiger remarked about World War I. And articles began appearing which quite distorted the facts—I know, I know," Archer said, raising an admonishing hand, "what are facts?—but after all, if you are going to accuse a person of crimes they never dreamed of let alone committed on one hand, and praise them as the reincarnation of our Lord on the other—where was I?—in short, the heirs decided to have one biographer to start with and then let everyone say what they wanted after the facts, or what I call the facts, had been got in place, if possible with some grace and readability. I cannot think how I ever expected to get out of that sentence, or what you must think of my claims to grace in the face of such a lack of syntax. And of course," he added, concluding with a certain flourish, "we are two biographers, but you will have taken my point."

"I have taken it," Kate said, "and am intrigued. And what can I do for you at the moment to help with the biography?"

They had reached the dessert stage, which in a Chinese restaurant, unless one is given to kumquats, oranges, or ice cream, means that one is finished. But there are always fortune cookies. "Have you noticed," Kate asked, opening a cookie to extract her fortune, "how even the most severely rational among us still cling to the idea of some presence somewhere who knows all and will guide us? Nothing could keep me from consulting my fortune cookie, nor, if it applies even remotely, heeding it to some slight extent, though I know what nonsense it all is. We all like to see a pattern in our lives, and to call it destiny, and to think that some sentient being wiser than ourselves guided that destiny and offers hints about it from time to time. 'You should seize the next opportunity that offers itself.' There, you see what I mean: the message from beyond this messy existence. Why this disquisition on fortune cookies? Because I had the sense that Patrice, for reasons I couldn't begin to tell you, was in danger of interpreting the fog in the airport as one interprets a fortune cookie, that is to say, to see in it enlightenment, encouragement, recognition of one's needs. That, I think, is why, so oddly, she asked me if I believed in God. And in a sense, I now realize, I understood her; I think my referring to Mrs. Ramsay's phrase shows that. I understood her need to believe there is a plan somehow, as Mrs. Ramsay needed that belief, that wish that we might be in the hands of the Lord. It is a belief that not even so conventional a woman Mrs. Ramsay could sustain. Can any of this possibly matter? Can it possibly help?"

There was a pause. "It helps," Herbert said. "You know, I imagine, that Patrice committed suicide. Archer is puzzling over that. You see, Archer knew Patrice, which I did not. He found her wholly lovable. Archer adores eccentricity: he adores people who, like oil paintings, are only one of a kind."

"Provided," Archer added in his frivolous way, "they are not unbearably intense and without humor; you know, committed to things like vegetarianism or the dangers of tooth plaque. People can use dental floss

8

all they like, but they oughtn't to make a crusade out of it. Like jogging, if you follow me.''

"Oh, quite easily," Kate said.

"Well," Herbert continued, "I never knew Patrice. I had to learn about her from all the documents, the writings, the letters, the journal, above all from those who knew her, who loved her, who hated her (there were more than a few, of course), and I have come up with a rather different person from Archer's—not incompatible, but different. I believe that Patrice's can be an exemplary life, a legend, they would have said in the Middle Ages. Like Donne, I think that lovers make better legends than do saints."

"But of course," Kate said. "Do you think she decided to ask me about God because I drank Laphroaig? Surely such a drink bespeaks a proper skepticism. You must both come and drink some with my husband and me one evening soon. Will you?"

"With pleasure, my dear lady. Name the evening. What, by the way, does your husband do?"

"He tries to convict murderers of their crimes; no connection with Patrice. But I think you'll like him."

Chapter 2

> *Only in our virtues are we original, because virtue is difficult. . . . Vices are general, virtues are particular.*
>
> IRIS MURDOCH

*W*hile waiting for Archer and Herbert to arrive for the promised drink, Reed offered Kate a martini.

"Do you know," Kate said, "lately people have been telling me we drink too much. Do you think we do?"

"Of course. Shall we have straight vodka, as Balanchine did, or pretend we're making martinis? Any day now we'll take up white wine, since everyone else seems on the verge of deserting it for the hard stuff."

"In fact, I rather promised them Laphroaig; ought we perhaps to begin as we mean to go on?"

"Of course. If only all major decisions were so readily resolved. What are they like, your mysterious biographers? Apart from what I shall soon see for myself."

"I've just had a note from Archer today," Kate said. "He sends what he calls an encyclopedic account of Patrice's life. He writes: 'We all know this tells us nothing or less than nothing, yet by these "facts" she will be placed for you in a certain way. Herbert and I had expected only to consult with you once about your great airport meeting with herself, but now we wonder if we might not impose outrageously to discuss some of our really big questions with you also. I shan't say we ask this because you are a woman, but perhaps because you are a certain kind of woman, not defensive about the "expected" woman's life. (You will know very well what I mean, dear Kate, and will not take offense.)' He and Herbert look forward to seeing me and the enviable Reed. . . ."

"He sounds a bit fey," Reed said, "which may be either delightful or trying, depending on the chap."

"Delightful, I do assure you. Archer lives his life as though he were entrapped in a Cole Porter lyric, and like Cole Porter's lyrics, his life looks easier to achieve than it is."

"And have you read the encyclopedic article on Patrice's life?"

"Only glanced at it, but far enough to discover that her husband was killed in a mugging."

"Good heavens, I *thought* I'd heard that singular name Umphelby before, but it wouldn't jog into place. We prosecuted the case downtown. Two teenage boys who killed him with a gun when he tried to stop them stealing his watch; he'd given them his wallet. Sheer idiotic stubbornness, of course, but oh lord! We got the kids, for what it was worth. If they hadn't had a gun . . . but why start on that. How horrible for her, which must be the aspect of it all you'll be considering together with Archer and Herbert. And there, I think, they are."

Neither Archer nor Herbert was a drinker of anything but wine in the ordinary way: like anyone who might be compared to a Cole Parter lyric, however, Archer understood the need for significant libations, and Herbert followed Archer's social clues. They drank a toast to Patrice and her biography with the straight stuff to which they had added a little cool water such as

11

had not, Kate pointed out, been available at that dreadful airport.

"I've just learned," Reed said, "that Patrice Umphelby's husband was killed in a mugging. Such an event must loom large in anyone's biography, I should think."

"It does of course," Herbert said. "It marks a change in her life; after her period of grief and mourning a profound switch, such as one finds often in those who have been close to death. One's whole scale of what is important seems to shift: social niceties fade, those conversations and events which offer intensity matter more. Life becomes both more and less valuable. It's one of the hardest things to get down in this biography, and, as you might guess," Herbert smiled at Kate, "everytime I try, Archer looks pained and fears the worst in the way of a religious disquisition."

"Christopher Isherwood once said of Auden," Archer said, "that when they were writing plays together, Isherwood had to keep a close eye on Auden, or the characters would fall to their knees. We're in an analogous situation."

"You've lost me," Reed said. "One moment we were discussing a mugging and grief, and the next religious conversion. Have I missed something, or is this one of those leaps of faith that people in Kate's line of work are always making. Do you follow, my dear?"

"I think Herbert means that, after her husband's sudden and violent death, Patrice became another person. But one does not become a wholly other person; only the person one had the power to be should life deliver the necessary brutal shove."

"Is the shove always brutal?" Archer asked. "Something in my happy-go-lucky nature objects to so grim a view of destiny."

"Grim or not," Herbert said, "what Archer is sticking at is my belief that if the word means anything, Patrice was a saint."

"Lordy," Kate said. "I'm with Archer. How I hate saints."

"That," Herbert said, "is because you imagine them like Mother Teresa, she of the child-care project in India and the Nobel Prize."

"Exactly. She spoke at a Harvard commencement or class day or something and declared that abortion was the greatest sin of all, in the next breath urging the young of both sexes to remain virgins till they married. Well, in one view, I suppose, it requires the conviction of sainthood to urge virginity upon undergraduates these days, let alone at Harvard."

"I simply refuse," Archer interjected, "to imbibe thoughts of sainthood together with this glorious Laphroaig. That you and Patrice, my dear Kate, once let it lead you to God is as much religious effect as we should require of this innocent beverage. Poor Herbert is trying to find a new definition of sainthood which combines inconsistency, generosity, the willingness to take risks, and service to ideals beyond one's own immediate demands. I don't call it sainthood, as I have told the dear boy time and time again: I call it successful middle age. Advanced middle age. And that, together with a sudden and unsought solitude, was what our Patrice was coping with. Saints are a fraud by definition: once called saints, they cease to be, in my opinion. We know our saints only by the fact that their saintliness is unrecognized. *And that*," he concluded, "is the longest speech I have ever made on a religious subject in my life, the longest and, I promise you, the last."

Reed filled Archer's glass again. "Sainthood bores us," he said, "and that's a fact. But middle age: now there's a subject."

Kate stared at him.

"Well, my dear, as might be expected, I'm thinking of myself in darkest middle age, and wondering where now? I mean, as I have mentioned one or two times before, I'm growing rather long in the tooth for the DA's

13

office. Where next, I ask in middle age, what adventure, what possibility?''

"If I didn't know you so well," Kate remarked, "I'd say you had been drinking."

Smiling at her, Reed turned to Archer and Herbert. "I don't know how much you know about the DA's office; most people don't know much, and why should they? Most of the top senior trial lawyers there, in which exalted number I include myself, quit by their late thirties: and it's not just that the work is very demanding, requiring youthful energy and vigor. That's true even in corporate law. It's that after the first thousand rapes and murders, one knows how the system works. I've stayed on, like an ancient pitcher in the major leagues, called in for the close ones, and pulling it off yet once again. All right, all right," he said, in response to a grimace from Kate, "I don't want to make myself out as too pitiful an object. A highly skilled litigator I am, and hope always will be. But I've grown more interested in how the system works, individual rights versus getting the guilty, than in each individual case. There's the whole question of how police forces can function in a democracy and in countries hoping to be democracies. It's not a simple problem: one is likely to veer too far one way or the other."

"Are you involved in the big cases at the DA's office?" Archer asked. "The Abbott case, Son of Sam, that sort of thing?"

"That sort of thing exactly," Reed said. "And what can it be about your magic Patrice that has me discussing all this with two people I never met before?"

"To say nothing of springing it on your wife," Kate laughed. "Not that I haven't had my suspicions, what with you running off to the ends of the earth all the time, advising developing countries."

"I understand perfectly why you mention this in connection with Patrice," Herbert said. "She had a theory about middle age. She thought of it as a time quite different from the earlier years, cut off from the

14

ghosts of the past. One might recall those ghosts; most people, she thought, recall them too often. But they need no longer haunt one. You have the sense she spoke of, of life able to begin again, if one will but let it.''

"And, I suppose," Reed said, "if one is not only willing to admit to being middle aged, but proud of it.''

"You only say that because you're slightly younger than I am," Kate added, "which I will never forgive you for, idiotic as I know that to be.''

"Rot," Reed said, reaching out to touch her. "But your Patrice's theories of middle age intrigue me. Is that why she is worthy of a biography, because she held new theories of middle age? What was she a professor of, anyway?''

"History, in fact," Herbert said. "But by the end she had become famous as what I fear we must call a personality, and, of course, as a writer.''

"I'm afraid I never heard of her," Reed said, "probably because Kate didn't talk about her work. What did she write?''

"Several important history books, in the earlier years, including one that made quite a splash at the time. It was called *The Years Between*, and was, as you would expect, an account of the years between the world wars. She also wrote what is probably the best book on World War I literature, which tends to show that she was lapping over from history into Kate's world, in a way. But what made her famous was her fiction. About ten years before her death she began writing stories and novels, almost all of which were published first in *The New Yorker*. She developed quite a following, even what they called a cult—''

"But as you no doubt know," Archer interjected, "they always call admirers a cult when the admired writer is a woman; if one admires Virginia Woolf or Stevie Smith or Sylvia Plath, one is part of a cult. If one writes endlessly on James Joyce, one is just showing good business sense.''

"My favorite of her books," Herbert said, "is one called *The Years of the Red Cat*. It's part fantasy, part astute social commentary, about a spinster who becomes a witch."

"Ah," Reed said. "And her advice to me would be, go thou and do likewise. I take it being a spinster is not a necessary condition."

"The thing about her writing," Archer said, "is that she never preached. She appealed both to intellectuals and to those who dream alone in small towns and suburbs. There are great hopes that our biography will sell, and all her books in even larger numbers after it." Archer paused a moment. "We can deal with all that," he said. "And if I watch Herbert carefully, we can deal with what I shall have to cure him of calling her sainthood. The problem really is her death."

"There is the fact," Kate said, "that she killed herself. Is that the problem?"

"Partly. She walked into the lake at Clare College, where she taught. It was in June, the time of graduation. The place was swarming with women come back for class reunions. It caused quite a stir."

"There is, then, no doubt," Reed asked, "that she walked in voluntarily; that she did, in fact, *walk* in?"

"None whatever, alas. But it isn't just the suicide that makes our book difficult, at the moment; and the book has, as you may have gathered, stuck a bit. It's because of her journal and what to do with that. I thought you might look at it," he said to Kate. "And you, also, of course," he added to Reed.

"What did she say in the journal?" Reed asked. "If I walk into a lake, you shall know it was hankypanky?"

"Nothing like that," Herbert said. "You see. . ." Herbert paused a minute, as though considering how to express his thought.

"Put it as she put it in the journal," Archer said. "She was in love with death."

It was a few days later that Kate and Reed, again reverting to Laphroaig, for which they seemed to have developed a sudden affection ("Certain to be better for one than martinis," they told each other), spoke again of Patrice. Kate had read the encyclopedic facts provided by Archer and Herbert. Most of the dramatic facts had, of course, already been covered. Patrice had had two children, still living, for whom she had had a great affection, greatly reciprocated. She had been a professor of history; her specialty had been Europe in the last hundred years, particularly between the so-called world wars. In recent years before her death, as well as writing successful stories and novels, she had lectured widely around the country and conducted faculty seminars; she had become quite a well-known figure without ever being a famous product as our public relations world understands fame. She was fifty-eight when she died.

Kate paused to do some arithmetic. "She was forty-nine when her husband was killed, which was after she had begun writing. Archer has promised to send the journal, and that, I dare say, will tell us more about her than these bare facts. She has begun to fascinate me, this Patrice Umphelby. And as always happens when you begin thinking about something or someone, you find it everywhere. It amazes me now that I didn't stumble over Patrice at every turn while she was still alive. And yet, we met each other only that once in the airport. It's odd, really, that she should have spoken of God, and that Herbert should have this sense of her as saintlike, at any rate, as spiritually out of the ordinary."

"Your addiction has affected even me," Reed said. "I actually asked them up in Massachusetts to get me all the facts they could about Patrice's death. More, as you know, gets stashed away in police files than ever is told to the mourning survivors."

"You *were* suspicious," Kate said. "You don't believe she walked into that lake."

"I wondered. However in love with death she was,

her suicide didn't seem to fit the picture Herbert and Archer were painting for us. But it's all as recounted in the press at the time: she put rocks into her pockets and walked, or swam, to the middle of the lake. She might have done that, of course, because she knew that one day she would become a matter of interest to you, and people of interest to you always behave in amazing ways, but if that's the explanation, it's the only available one. She hadn't been hit, drugged, nor had she drunk much: just an ounce or two of whiskey. She died of drowning, as she had planned to, in the middle of the night. She left a note in her living room, a message for her children. This said that they had always agreed with her about the death of Charlotte Perkins Gilman, whom she quoted, and she knew they would understand. Charlotte Perkins Gilman was the biggest puzzle at the time; it took the police longer to figure out who she was than the whole rest of the case put together. They finally were led to a professor in California named Carl Degler, who identified Charlotte Perkins Gilman and told them she had killed herself with chloroform. Patrice's children were saddened, but not duly surprised by their mother's death. They had expected it to come later, but they knew her views on old age, which were not benign. Still, fifty-eight seemed much too young. Carl Degler had written an introduction to a book by Charlotte Perkins Gilman called *Women and Economics*, which is how the police were led to him; it was suggested that the book might reveal more facts relevant to Patrice's death, but apparently it didn't. And that's all there is to that. The college, needless to say, wished that Patrice had used chloroform instead of their lake, for which one can hardly blame them.''

Kate stretched her legs out onto the coffee table and looked at Reed. ''I'm still wondering what to make of the other night,'' she said. ''It seemed unlike you, mentioning a personal problem first in front of others.

And then I let out the shameful fact that you're younger than I am. I've been worrying, rather, ever since."

"I too, my love, and I apologize. Blame it on your Patrice Umphelby. But I shall have to make a move, you know. And I found it somehow inspiring to consider that middle age might be more than the playing out of repressed childhood needs. I liked her ideas about life at middle age."

"I, too. Have you any thoughts what you shall do?"

"A few. I don't of course want to spend my life in a part of the world where you are not; that's some of the problem."

"Reed, does it make sense to leave a job you like and do well, and respect yourself for doing, just because no one else holds it after the age of forty? It hasn't begun to bore you, has it?"

"No one could call it boring. What can I say? There comes a moment, as who knows better than you, when one has to move forward, when it is impossible to stay in the same place without moving back. I think it's because I can't explain myself any better than that that I've resisted talking of it, even to you. But I would have, soon enough, as you know."

"Odd that Patrice should have had that effect on you the other evening. I suspect it is the sort of effect she had on certain people, and on many received opinions. I can't help worrying, though you mustn't tell Archer and Herbert I said so, if she isn't one of those people who become a sort of divine dazzle when recalled after their death, but who may be a bit hard to live with on a day-to-day basis. Great intensity and originality may be hard to take as a steady diet."

"Perhaps. Nothing worthwhile is easy as a steady diet. But she does resonate, your Patrice. I'm eager to hear about the journal."

"She does fascinate me, Reed. I wonder why?"

"And I wonder why you're trying to fight that fascination. I think you love her, Kate. Why not just let that

19

be. You can't really mind her goading me into saying before her biographers what I should only have said first to you alone?''

''Reed, you are a beast to say that; you are also a remarkably perspicacious man. Have I mentioned it lately?''

Chapter 3

> *When she realized she would be alone, she threw away every*
> *assumption she had learned and began at zero. First off, she*
> *cut her hair. That was one thing she didn't want to think*
> *about anymore. Then she tackled the problem of trying to*
> *decide how she wanted to live and what was valuable to her.*
> *When am I happy and when am I sad and what is the*
> *difference? What do I need to know to stay alive? . . .*
> *[S]ince death held no terrors for her (she often spoke to the*
> *dead), she knew there was nothing to fear.*
>
> TONI MORRISON

*K*ate opened Patrice's journal. "Whenever I read the story or autobiography of an older woman," it began:

"Whenever I read the story or autobiography of an older woman—and they are rare enough—I find that though it is written by a woman in her fifties or beyond, she writes only to go back to her youth; she abandons age, experience, wisdom, to search the past, usually for romance, always for the beginnings in childhood. The important event always begins: 'And then I met this man.' (Unless it takes the form, 'God called to me.') Virginia Woolf wrote a rare novel of a woman in her fifties, but Woolf was a genius. I am an intelligent woman of fifty-five, and all the story I have is in the present. I note that I am already older than Clarissa Dalloway, who had just broken into her fifty-second year.

"I shall not go back. Of course, there will be memory. The past arises, or is caught for a moment in an event, a smell (how often I notice that), a sound like waves or a train whistle, a place which suddenly presents the past to us, complete. But such a moment shall not serve me as the excuse to tell the story of my youth. I do not find a story there. And for me, stories of youth are tired stories. But the story of age, of maturity before infirmity, before meaningless old age, has never been told. Except perhaps by Shakespeare, who told everything, provided he could tell it of men.

"Woolf wrote: 'Those moments—in the nursery, on the road to the beach—can still be more real than the present moment. This I have just tested.' And she reports how the sensations of her childhood seem to live perhaps independently of her, and to be recalled with an intensity available only in childhood. Not that I deny the truth of this for her or others. It is not true for me. Not only am I devoid of nostalgia, I seem devoid of memory, of all but its sudden, quickly vanishing assaults. And what I do remember is not memory, but a potted narrative, a story, like the story of the birth of my children, readily available as anecdote because I have got it pat. What I tell, of course, is not the past but the story I have made of the past, which encloses it and saves me from reinterpretation. Surely I cannot be the only woman in her fifties who lives in the present alone.

"Heidegger has said that we move between the 'no longer' and the 'not yet.' For me, the years ahead must be devoted to the 'not yet,' to what has not yet come into being in the world. But if I am without nostalgia, I am also without long-range personal hope. I observe how everyone deludes herself, himself, about old age. Each thinks old age will be bearable in that one case. I have never met an old person I enjoyed for more than a minute, if truth be told, and if truth not be told, why write here? Oh, maybe their stories are all right the first time you hear them, particularly if the old people have known the famous or done brave things. But they repeat themselves like tapes on a tape deck when the right button is pushed to turn on the prerecorded story. No, for me the life that matters extends from twenty-five to seventy, and I am in the last decades of it. The Old Testament was right about this at least: the proper span of human life is three score years and ten. I have saved pills, or I shall walk into the ocean, or one of these new diseases that confound the immunologists will find me, and I shall be careful that it is not detected in time for life-extending methods. Such summons to death can, I believe, be considered only before the last decade of the meaningful life.

"Stevie Smith felt as I do, I think; as she wrote to a friend, 'Here I was thinking of my next, and going to call it Married to Death, I'm nuts on death really, it comes out in my poems and does something to limit their ready sale . . . . But this death idea, it is very prominent, rather a running-away in my case I am afraid, not very *strrrong* of me. . . . But there it is, death death death lovely death. . . .' But I must remember that she tried suicide, that in the end she died of a brain tumor, still in her sixties, and that she celebrated, mockingly to be sure, the tedium of domestic work: "I just stay at home and get absolutely fascinated by doing the same thing at the same time over and over again every day. I should be quite lost without it.'

"For Woolf, for me, it is quite different, 'A great part of every day is not lived consciously,' Woolf wrote. 'One walks, eats, sees things, deals with what has to be done.' She lists the things, all domestic: dinner, a broken vacuum cleaner. And Woolf admitted to herself that 'when it is a bad day the proportion of non-being is much larger'; for the moments of intensity, of being, are embedded in many more moments of nonbeing. But I have discovered, as it is clear Woolf had discovered, that if one lives with enough intensity, there are more moments of being. And the moments of nonbeing inherent in idle chatter, dinner parties, meetings

23

where nothing is said, greetings where no response is desired, can be disdained. Still, moments of non-being, like housework, are cherished for the moments of being they provide a needed rest from. Yet I think that it is not quite what Stevie Smith meant. I think that, even though she was not old then, like the old everywhere, she preserved her life by a routine of 'the tedium of domestic work.'

"I have had, as the French say with their marvelous accuracy, a *coup de vieux*. I have faced the fact that I am old nor will I bury that realization in tedium, or the assurances of my family and ancient friends that I exist because they need to believe it, because they too need to believe that they will exist when old. I recognize that there is something about aging the human mind cannot take in, certainly not in youth, perhaps never. What young woman believes she will ever grow heavy and have wrinkles and thin hair? I think I was born into the revelation of being old, had my *coup de vieux*, because I was, in a way, born again. A critic writing the introduction to Richardson's *Pamela*, has mentioned that novels, like journals, tend to be about adolescence because we like to observe the struggle of a person to become a self. But has it ever been suggested, except of course by Woolf, that a novel might be written about a woman in her fifties who is, because of the lack of choice in women's lives when they are young, undergoing the very struggle my critic calls adolescent? Anyone reading this will say, of course, that I am depressed, which is why no one must read it. Who is there who can understand that I am full of joy. I have fallen in love with death, and love, if one does not pursue the object incontinently, is joyous. I hope I shall be able, at the proper time, to cry with Stevie Smith, 'Oh Sweet Death, come to me.' "

Kate put the journal down: it was indeed an extraordinary document. She heard again Archer's words: "You see, my dear, Patrice fell in love with death

sometime in her early fifties, and Herbert and I are unclear of what to do with this astonishing fact.''

What worried Archer and Herbert, Kate knew, was
not only how to write the biography of a woman who
spoke so bluntly of death and felt she had begun really
to live her life after the point when most people consider
life over. They were also deeply troubled that, in speaking honestly of Patrice's love of death, of her knowledge
of how death gave intensity to middle age as passion
and hope gave intensity to youth, they might mislead
the young. Archer and Herbert were afraid that every
discouraged young person would take Patrice's welcome of the idea of death as an invitation to youthful
suicide, and that would be a terrible thing indeed. For
suicide in youth and at seventy are as different as are a
youthful woman and a woman of seventy. They wanted
Patrice to sound sane, which above all she was, and
they feared to lead anyone astray. A *coup de vieux*, Kate
thought, who had ever seen it as an opportunity for
life?

But, it turned out, serious as this problem was, it
was not what was worrying Archer and Herbert half
out of their minds. They turned up the next day,
having decided, as they put it, to come clean. Even
the most distant of restaurant tables held the risk of
eavesdroppers. ''Humpty Dumpty's listener down
chimneys is everywhere,'' Archer said. So they met
in Kate's office.

''The problem is,'' Kate said, ''I feel like someone
you have come to consult professionally.''

''Got it in one,'' Archer said, rather uncharacteristically. ''Damn,'' he added. ''Okay, here goes. We have
for some time been fearing that Patrice was murdered.'' Kate, staring at him, began to recover the sensations she had felt in that fog-bound airport long ago.
Laphroaig, of course, was out of the question and out of
reach. It was two o'clock in the afternoon.

''I am not professionally a private eye,'' Kate said.
''I thought you wanted to consult me because I was an

25

unusual woman," she rather sadly added. "Besides," and she sat back with a sigh of relief, tilting her chair in a manner suitable to a private eye, "Reed looked into it, and she wasn't murdered. Not unless someone dragged her out to the lake, leaving no signs of struggle, having drugged her with something unknown to modern medicine. He got the plain facts from the local police in Massachusetts, I do assure you. You've both been working too hard," she finished in consoling tones.

Herbert leaned forward toward Kate, and his worried face brought her up slowly from her tilt. "We don't mean, Kate, that she was literally murdered. She entered the lake herself; she chose to die. The question is, why then, why that way?"

"But she had fallen in love with death," Kate said. "I read it myself in her journal. You gave it to me."

"She meant, as you well know," Herbert said, "that as the hope of an unending future (as it seems to youth) makes the risks of youth possible, so the hope of death, if needed, makes the risks of middle age possible. But she spoke of the biblical age of seventy, three score years and ten. She was only fifty-eight, with every reason to go on with her life, and with the risks that were turning out so well."

"But," Kate said, "when you fall in love, you are in danger of being seduced."

"And that's what you think happened?" Archer asked. "Even you, whom life, one could reasonably guess, has trained to suspicion? So would not someone who wished her ill be able to count on everyone thinking just that? That she had been seduced by death?"

Not, it turned out the following Friday morning, quite everyone. Kate who had, in her opinion, been designed by destiny to sleep until noon, achieved her fate only on Fridays, and then only on those Fridays when her university had not decided to hold some meeting or other. Kate's response to an early morning meeting had been Tallulah Bankhead's on being invited somewhere at nine in the morning. "Oh," she is supposed to have replied in wonder, "are there *two* nine o'clocks in the day?"

It was barely ten when Reed, who had been working at home, roused her for the telephone. "The president of Clare College is on the phone," Reed said, "or at any rate ready to leap to the phone when you are safley on this end. Her secretary sounded imperative; they called originally at nine, and I suggested a later hour. Perhaps you'd better talk to her."

"Someone's idea of a beastly joke," Kate said ungraciously.

"Trust me, my love. She may be calling only to ask you to donate something grand to the new college recreational center, but it is the president, I promise you."

Kate said "hello" to herself rapidly up and down the scale to make her voice sound less sleepy, and then "hello" into the phone. "Just a moment, please, Professor Fansler. President Norton to speak to you."

"Professor Fansler, good morning. Sorry to bother you at home, but I'm calling on a rather delicate matter. Have you a moment to discuss it now? How kind of you. I don't believe we've ever met. But Madeline Huntley has spoken so highly of you. She's here for the year, you know, running our new Jackson Center."

"No," Kate said, feeling some response was required. "I didn't know. I thought she was in private practice in Boston."

"We persuaded her to run our institute in its all-important first year. She's been kindness itself in supporting me through our little troubles. And she suggested that you might be the answer. We all, that is the trustees and I, put our thinking caps on and decided the solution might be to appoint you to our task force on the question of Gender Studies. If you would be so good. It meets only every other week."

"But I hardly think . . ."

"Your advice would be valuable, of course," President Norton interrupted, "but the task force would only be what the spy novels call your cover. You would really be here to look into Patrice Umphelby's death. People," President Norton added, her voice clearly indicating the sort of dissidents describable as *people*, "have begun asking questions and spreading doubt. We thought it best to nip it in the bud. You are helping with the biography," (the president ignored a small yelp of protest from Kate), "and have had experience in investigations. You seemed ideal, therefore, and I call to ask if you will do us the great favor of joining our task force? We can talk more about your undercover work when you arrive. Perhaps you would like to think it over."

Kate, who had been leaning on her elbow in bed, fell back upon the pillows. Why think it over? The voice asking was not President Norton, but Patrice who had shared Kate's malt liquor in a fog-bound airport. One may love death, but that hardly gave death the right to kill one. Kate chuckled. "I don't have to think it over," she said. "I'll serve on your task force. Will you write me a letter about that?"

"Of course. And there will be a small honorarium."

"All right then. But please remember, President Norton, I may not be Clare College's idea of a lady. I read the memoirs of John Kenneth Galbraith a few years ago, and when he suggested that the women students be considered as future professionals, and not as just wives and mothers, he reported that the most fearsome enemies of change at Radcliffe were the women trustees. Why should women be prepared for professional careers, they asked him; what else is as important as being a good wife and mother? I mention this only because I have a feeling your trustees are probably from the same mold and may not take to me. I have," Kate announced, now fully awake, "been called a feminist."

"That," President Norton said, "is why we want you for the task force. A countervailing force. Do let me know when you can come and talk to me, Professor Fansler. I look forward to it. And so, I'm certain, will many others."

Hanging up the phone, Kate thought she understood President Norton well enough. That dangerous feminist, Kate Fansler, would find, as was inevitable, that Patrice Umphelby had committed suicide in an unhappily prominent and thoughtless way. Kate had met Patrice, but had not known her intimately: in every way qualified for the job, Kate thought; the whitewash from such a one will stick. But, Kate thought, I shall quote them Hawthorne, the self-satisfied fools. Even if Patrice did commit suicide, why should she have done it then, before she had always meant to? Having at last risen from bed, showered, and faced the fact that the day had begun, Kate went in search of Hawthorne and read the passage to Reed:

"He's talking," she explained, "about when he lost his job at the custom house: 'In view of my previous weariness of office, and vague thoughts of resignation, my fortune somewhat resembled that of a person who should entertain an idea of committing suicide, and, altogether beyond his hopes, meet with the good hap to be murdered.' But was it in this case a good hap? I doubt it, dear President Norton, I doubt it very much."

"Do bear in mind, my love," Reed said, "that Patrice probably walked into the lake of her own free will, as all the available evidence suggests."

"I can't wait to hear what Madeline Huntley has to say," Kate answered. "It's very unlike her to head an institute."

"And very like you," Reed remarked, "to be part of a task force. Perhaps you should leave off teaching and I the DA's office, and we should form a firm of private detectives, academic cases our specialty."

29

"You always become unpleasant when I join distant task forces," Kate mused.

"I'll miss you," Reed said. "I always do."

Chapter 4

I do not know which makes a man more conservative—to know nothing but the present, or nothing but the past.
JOHN MAYNARD KEYNES

*C*lare College, like all of the eastern women's colleges, including those once called the Seven Sisters (a name recently commandeered, like so much else, by the major oil companies) had its great period between the end of World War I and the end of the Vietnam War. All the brightest and the best women went to such schools, or enough to gain great reputation for these colleges. In 1974 Elizabeth Tidball published an analysis of the educational patterns of women of achievement, and discovered that a high proportion of those women who had gone on to become professionals with advanced degrees and a measure of success in the world had attended an all-women college, usually a prestigious one in the East. Wellesley College was so impressed by this report that it gave Elizabeth Tidball an honorary degree. But by the end of the seventies much had changed, including the admission of women to all the major universities and colleges that had been formerly all male. It was too early to tell how these women

31

would do, compared to those who still attended women's colleges with all their advantages, above all a faculty at least half women, and the chance to hold all student offices and not to worry about men while being intellectually impressive. But the suspicions were beginning to take hold that the women's colleges had somehow missed their chance to continue to be impressive. Kate had always believed in women's colleges, in the important chance for women to spend four years having to themselves all the experience and attention that were to be got on their college campus, and which is far more readily given to men if men are present. But even Kate had begun to wonder about the viability of women's colleges, and this idea was now gaining interest for her as she thought more about Patrice, her life and death. Having, therefore, arrived for her first meeting of the task force and her first conference with the president, she found herself, after taking the shuttle to Boston, being met at the airport by her old acquaintance Madeline Huntley. Kate asked her, after the proper greeting, what in the name of psychiatry she was doing at Clare College.

"Trying to convince the students that depression and guilt are not sins committed only by the radical left, but human experiences it is really all right to admit to. They will grant that they have an eating problem, and perhaps even allow as how maybe they are a bit too anxious about grades, but suggest that they have any anger, or are ever depressed, and you are up against the protestant ethic and old-fashioned ideas about sin. You wouldn't believe."

"But what is this institute, and why are you running it?"

"Some man named Jackson, the widower of an alumma, gave funds for our new institute. It's called an institute only because it has to be called something, and the funds, as always, while generous, are insufficient. The institute is supposed to deal with the problems of students and faculty as women. The only thing you aren't allowed to mention, it transpires, is that any of them might feel any profound responses because they are women. We aren't supposed to admit that there are any disadvantages to being a woman in our world today.''

"It sounds like Phyllis Schlafly. Do you think the atom bomb was a gift of God?"

"It's not that bad; they're for disarmament, on the whole, and saving the environment, in so far as they've figured out what that entails. They certainly want to stop the Japanese from killing whales. But they have a deep, inherent suspicion toward suggestions that the patriarcal structure (I whisper the phrase for your ears alone) has imposed on them in any way, or ought to change in any way, or that family is not a word encompassing all virtue, nor itself the bulwark against all evil, and they feel most of that is propounded by shrill feminists, otherwise known as women's libbers. Do you want the whole litany?''

"Do you know?" Kate said, "whenever I visit Boston and someone meets me at the airport, I always have my most relaxed conversations of the whole visit while stuck in a traffic jam in the Callahan Tunnel. But surely women's colleges should be more aware of the problems of womanhood than most?''

"Should be, but aren't. There are lots of explanations for this, and mine, if you care, is that the alumnae are all such ladies, calling themselves Mrs. John Jones III, and they would consider it unladylike in the extreme to suggest that women be other than helpmates and volunteers, when they aren't being wives and mothers. I know it sounds old hat but it's still the truth. Not one New England women's college testified before Congress on behalf of the ERA, of dear dead memory, or has taken any stand whatever on behalf of women's rights. The result is that they are far behind the formerly all-male colleges in everything from women's studies to public stands on battered wives.''

"I just don't get it," Kate said. "Maybe it's the

33

fumes in the tunnel, but I don't get it. Surely they've given honorary degrees to some outstanding women who might be called feminists."

"Smith has; not Clare. Smith has given honorary degrees to Betty Friedan and Gloria Steinem—well, they went to Smith—but they also gave one to Adrienne Rich, who didn't. Clare never gave Patrice Umphelby an honorary degree, or even a pat on the shoulder. Because all along she kept saying disturbing things, and being *unladylike!* I know, by the way, that you've come about Patrice Umphelby's death, so don't give me any folderol about task forces. And look, don't take my word for any of this: just hang around a few days, say after your task force meets. Or better still, offer to give a talk entitled 'Why Women Today Should Be Angry.' It will be attended by a small group of radical students, a few nontenured women professors who are feminists, teach courses called, with a not-so-refined sneer, women's studies, and have been ostracized by their departments who don't consider them sound scholars, and a few administrators who would like to blow the whole place up, metaphorically speaking, but can't risk their jobs. No professor of either sex will come, and the English department will hold a compulsory department meeting at the same time as your talk. The college newspaper will write up your visit as though you were a crank who was probably suffering from shingles, hemorrhoids, and male rejection, which is why you are sounding that way. I'm sure that's the treatment Patrice got."

"Madeline, let me get this straight." Since they were standing still in the tunnel, Madeline was able to look at Kate upon this request, removing her sunglasses. "You are a prominent psychoanalyst and doctor; how did you get here, and what, after all, seems to be the matter? Are you all right, really?"

"You see what I mean!" Madeline explained triumphantly, edging forward three feet. "You've known me, how many years? Ten at least. We've talked about
34

everything under the sun, and served on endless committees and panels to confront problems and disperse funds and fellowships. But the minute I begin describing dear old Clare, with its ivy-covered walls and rolling meadows, its repressed and unhappy students, and its reactionary and fearful faculty, you decide that I've undergone a personal disaster, and require careful nurturing."

"Your point is taken. But I still don't know why you're working there, if you think the place is so awful."

"I'm temporary, till they find someone to run their institute, which is about as much an institute as I'm a brain surgeon. I hold court in a patient's room in the infirmary, and have to fight with everyone else for secretarial help and the use of the Xerox machine. They even tried to charge the rent for the patient's room to the institute at the rate they would charge an actual patient. I thought it would be interesting to find out about women at a women's college, and I was right, it is interesting in a horrible way, the way war is interesting. Also, the people at the research center convinced me that if I didn't take the job, some male Freudian who still thought all women suffered from penis envy would. As Patrice would have said, we in middle age require adventure. Next time I'll join a convent and be done with it. Ah, Storrow Drive at last. We've got to get on the Mass Turnpike and then ride for a half hour or more, so relax my dear, and tell me what you're up to. Why are you suddenly here on the trail of dear Patrice? She's been dead almost a year, hasn't she?"

"Madeline, for pity's sake. I did promise President Norton that I'd keep my sleuthing mission a secret. I'm a genuine member of the task force. Are you just eager for any excitement you can find at Clare, or is there real gossip about Patrice's death?"

"The latter, my dear sleuth. It all started with Veronica Manfred, who will be confronting you, I doubt not, the minute you are available. Gossip spreads on this campus like mononucleosis. And after all, it isn't every day a renowned professor and writer of witty fantasy walks into the waters to drown herself. Even Virginia Woolf, and that was nearly fifty years ago, had a history of madness, or what was called madness. But dear Patrice, though eccentric, was as sane as an old boot. And how she ever lasted all those years at Clare, I'll never know. She was, no doubt, a wonderful teacher, of course.''

"You realize," Kate said, "that she almost certainly did commit suicide. I'm just here to satisfy my curiosity, really, and Archer's and Herbert's.''

"And who might they be?''

"Not another word, unless you want to turn around and go through the Callahan Tunnel again. I need to hear about the president of dear old Clare, since she and I meet tomorrow, and I've a feeling I'm going to be stroked and flattered into submission. I intend to be forthright and disagreeable, and I need some help from you. What's she like?''

"Let's put it this way: she's very young, early thirties, a lawyer, and smart, knows many of the right people, and would be fine if she were gutsy and on the right side. Unfortunately, she's neither, in my opinion, but you've already figured out that I'm prejudiced and my opinion isn't worth much. She certainly hasn't gone out on a limb for my institute, feeling we've already got a counseling service, and why emphasize the negative side of anything?''

"Oh, lord," Kate said.

The president of Clare had evidently decided that collegiality would be her note. She moved from behind her desk to sit with Kate on chairs grouped at the other end of the room. On this Kate gave her bad marks, just for starters; she was president of the college, speaking as president, and she ought to stay behind her damn desk. Kate had once visited a president at another women's college who, at lunch (which was held, to

Kate's extreme annoyance, in a cafeteria) had offered to get everyone coffee or tea. Kate understood that she was trying not to act like a businessman, but didn't see, also, why women shouldn't have the perks of the job. Surely, Kate had argued later, there was a middle ground between getting the coffee yourself and ordering your female secretary (whom you called the girl) to get it. No, she had been told, there wasn't. "I hate people pretending I'm their buddy when I'm not," Kate had said. The trouble with me, Kate reminded herself now, as she and the president sat knee to knee, is that I am irritable and fussy and don't want to be here. I bet she doesn't even smoke, and will mind if I do, but pretend not to.

"Do you mind if I smoke?" Kate said.

"Not at all," the president said, rising to search for an ashtray, an extended search that suggested the answer was almost always yes to that question. Which told Kate, who needed the information even more than she needed a cigarette, that the president needed *her*. She's got the wind up, Kate thought, beginning to enjoy herself.

"There are two items on our agenda," the president said, leaning back from Kate and trying hard not to fan the smoke away. Kate, taking pity, put out her cigarette: her aim had been, apart from nicotine longings, to observe the president, not to torture her. "First, of course, the task force upon which you have so generously agreed to serve. And second, the death of Patrice Umphelby. I thought we might take them up in reverse order."

"May I ask a question about the task force?"

"Certainly."

"Are you contemplating a Gender Studies program, or is the task force designed to discourage it?"

"I would hate to think we appointed a task force that considered itself preordained in any way. Still, I admit to seeing the force of your question. After all, you have served on university committees before."

"Many times," Kate said, as President Norton paused. "And many of them were honestly investigating, but all of them were stacked. Of course, some are unsuccessfully stacked, and human beings are not, thank heaven, inevitably predictable. But my experience, which is vast and has left me what I call knowledgeable or cynical depending on my mood, suggests that in this case you either intend to have a Gender Studies program but need the heft such a task force gives you, or you have decided against it and need to say that solution was the result of the careful investigation of many prominent and qualified people. The latter, may I hazard?"

"I see you like to go directly to the point; no shilly-shallying, no pretense."

"Nonsense," Kate replied. "I can shilly-shally as well as the next fellow, if it serves my purposes. I go straight to the point in this case because I haven't, as they say, an ax to grind. It is a matter of supreme indifference to me whether you have gender studies or not, since I know so little of the college. Shall we proceed to the far more problematic question of Patrice Umphelby? Once we've discussed that problem, you may decide you don't want me on the task force after all."

"That," President Norton said sadly, "is unlikely. To adopt your own direct method of discourse," she added with the first trace of humor Kate had glimpsed in her, "I don't want you here, but I need you. Someone has to get to the bottom of this, and you seem the obvious, the only one. I can't honestly say the prospect fills me with girlish eargerness."

"Well," Kate said, "I'm glad that's all said."

"You didn't, I think, know Patrice Umphelby?"

"We met once, in a airport, and talked about God. That meeting has somehow taken on all the significance of synecdoche, metonymy, and the force of the paradigmatic."

"Is that supposed to mean something, and if so what?"

"*Meaning* we do not strive for these days. We have taken a leaf from the French, and strive for theory, the better to impress you with. I did it rather well, don't you think? Paradigmatic significance aside, I did not know Patrice Umphelby, nor she me. I do, however, know something of her biographers."

"Yes. They seem to admire you."

"You know," Kate said, more gently than she had said anything hitherto, "you don't have to admire me in order for me to help you. You don't even have to like me. But you do have to trust me, up to a point. Can you, do you think? If not, I can be of no use, and will depart, no hard feelings, leaving you to your task force and whatever Umphelby ghosts are haunting you here."

President Norton rose and began to pace the room. Were I a lawyer, Kate thought, I would have developed the proper manner; she must have developed it, as a lawyer and as a president. But it's another matter to be the teller of tales we fear are disreputable. Kate waited in silence; if the woman chose to speak, she must do so in her own time, and without any new encouragement.

"It's odd, really," President Norton said. "I assured myself you could do no real harm on the task force, and I would decide whether or not to consult you on the Umphelby business after this conference. I suppose I planned to see if you were my sort of person. You're not, of course. And yet, I feel I can trust you, or at least, that I shall have to trust you, and that trusting you may not be a mistake."

"Why not tell me the problem? If we then discuss it and decide that I really will not do, I shall fold my tent like the Arabs and as silently steal way. Do you suppose Arabs still steal away silently, or have they become noisier in this technological age?"

President Norton sat down again. "Patrice Umphelby made a lot of trouble for the college even before her death. If you want to be Socratic and generous, you can say she was a gadfly; if you want to look at it from the point of view of the administration, she was a damn nuisance. Frankly, I think there was hardly a dean on campus, and at least half the faculty, who would not gladly have drowned her if they had had the chance. Yet, they are all mourning now, genuinely, I think, as though . . .'' She paused, perhaps deciding illumination did not lie that way.

"There was an administrator who spoke at her memorial service," Kate said. "She said she had disagreed with Patrice on everything, and had come to honor her, more, to understand how genuine were her actions."

"Can an action be not genuine?"

"It can be without thought, fulfilling an end that is selfishly necessary for psychological reasons rather than important for the community. I think the dean meant that she trusted Patrice's motives, and had even, to some extent, been persuaded by them."

"And what were they?" the president asked. "Disruption, the inducement of dissatisfaction, and turmoil?"

"Perhaps. Progress, or at least development, always looks like willful disruption at first and is certainly not seen as progress."

"Toward what was she progressing?"

"That," Kate said, "I cannot tell you. At least, not yet; perhaps never. Isn't that what you want to find out?"

"No. I want you to find out why she killed herself, and to settle the rumors forever. Or, if you begin to suspect that some mysterious method was used, unknown and undetectable poisons, mysterious oriental drugs, then we had better pursue that line. As it stands, Patrice is likely to be more trouble dead than alive, if I may put it with less than the usual grace expected of a president."

"I shall have to talk to people, poke around, make, like Patrice, a confounded nuisance of myself. Are you prepared for that?"

"I can hardly be prepared for what I so profoundly regret. But what is the alternative? I had a call this morning from a famous professor at the university where I used to teach at the law school. In those days I thought we agreed on most things, he and I. He is a philosopher and in charge of offering a joint degree in philosophy and law. I served on the law end. His recommendation counted strongly in my getting this job without having much administrative experience, and at an unusually early age. He, it seems, had met Patrice Umphelby at several conferences, and at some dinner they both attended, where they sat side by side and discussed death. Death was clearly the damn woman's favorite subject. She told him that she thought she or he would certainly be able to decide on the proper moment to die; the only problem would come from living past that moment. They promised, over what I suppose was a good deal too much wine with dinner, that they would inform the other if such a moment ever came to either of them. It's just the sort of damn-fool contract Umphelby was capable of entering into."

"I see," Kate said. "And she didn't call."

"Of course she didn't."

"Like women of my generation who promised to let a friend know when they first slept with someone. One usually was thinking of something else at the time."

The president deigned to smile. "Exactly. But it appears impossible to consider Umphelby as one would other people."

"I've heard her called a saint," Kate said. "Women saints, particularly around the time of Joan of Arc, seemed mostly to be burned, drowned, or, at the least, denounced. They spoke out, you see, against the church. Or the college."

"Was she religious?"

"I doubt it. I simply mean to imply that those who talk against institutions, particularly powerful and functioning institutions, are called damn nuisances by those in power, and saints after their death. Their one identifiable mark is that they make everyone uncomfortable. You do seem rather to have one of the species on your hands."

"Professor Fansler, I am a lawyer by training, not a student of religion. I am trying to run a college, which these days, as you probably know, means raising money and picking one's way delicately between the past and the future. There is no longer such a thing as a pure women's college, did you know that? They all have some men from nearby colleges around the place as students, and frequently the women rush off to some male or coed institution for further instruction. One nice scandal and a women's college today can be in trouble. Real trouble. People say, 'Who needs single-sex colleges at all? I might as well send my daughter to a coed college if there's scandal everywhere.'"

"I'll help if I can," Kate said. "I think you're seeing the business out of proportion. I understand the problem is publicity, and newspaper reporters are going to be on a campus murder, if there was a murder, as they were on to the killing of that Scarsdale doctor. You do have the option, you know, though I hardly need to tell you this, of sitting tight and letting the talk die down."

"You are my way of sitting tight. You are here to confer about the usefulness to the college of gender studies and, as an outside member of the task force, will naturally want to talk with many people. I'll send whomever you want to see a note, asking them to give you whatever help possible. Whom you choose to see is, of course, your decision; there is no one on the campus whose opinion would not be useful to the task force, unless we get down to consulting the grounds or kitchen staffs. Perhaps we can face that problem when we come to it."

"I'll have to come and go, of course," Kate said. "One has one's own commitments. But I'll do what I can. I think I'll find that Patrice was not murdered, but I may also be a problem about gender studies, once I've given my mind to it. Shall that be a dreadful inconvenience?"

"Dreadful. But yours will be only part of a large report."

"Perhaps I'll start with Patrice's department—history, wasn't it? Could I begin by seeing the women professors in that department?"

"There are no women professors in history," the president said. "Not tenured professors. Patrice was the only one. Why don't I give you a catalogue, and you can decide where you want to begin?"

"Is there someone named Veronica?" Kate asked.

"Lord, yes. But you don't have to seek her out. She's probably waiting for you at this very moment. Professor Fansler, I ought to thank you for all this, I know. We will, of course, try to arrive at a suitable honorarium."

Kate left this, as much else, in the air. The interview was over, and it was not clear that the president could have courteously borne another minute of it.

Chapter 5

The worthies of Clare are, it must be confessed, for so
maidenly a lodging, a motley crowd.
JOHN MAYNARD KEYNES

*K*ate, leaving the president's office in the administration building, found herself on a hill over-
looking parts of the campus and, beyond paths and
fields, the lake. This must have been one of the first
buildings erected when the college was begun, and it
still commanded a view designed to bring peace and a
sense of high purpose to the viewer. The lake was a
large one, and over the years the college had acquired
all the land surrounding it, so that no vulgar building
or activity offended the scholarly view. Kate understood it was a walk of several miles around the lake, and
she decided that such a walk would clear her brain and
perhaps jostle her thoughts into some order. Patrice
had liked to walk around the lake, her long strides taking her past more casual strollers on the narrow path.
Kate did not, of course, know this; in fact, she had just
made it up. But she had no doubt that time would
prove her right. Patrice was beginning to come alive for
her.

44

"Professor Fansler?" The man was leaning against one of the low walls extending from the building to the stairs Kate was about to descend. As he straightened up and came toward her she was aware that he had been there a longish time waiting for her, and that he had paused to see which way she would move. Kate, standing with her hands in her raincoat pockets, admitted her name.

"And yours?" she asked.

"Justine," he said. "Albert Justine. I am called, I like to think with singular inappropriateness, Bertie. I was a friend of Patrice's."

"Somehow," Kate said, "I thought you would be Veronica. Waiting for me, I mean. Does everyone know why I am here?"

"Everyone who cared for Patrice. That eliminates, just for example, most of the history department, and the entire departments of classics and English, at least their tenured contingent. I'm a professor of religion."

"How awkward," Kate said.

"You find religion awkward? That's a good sign. Too many people find it simply acceptable. Don't let my profession frighten you. I'm the John Mulmont Professor of New Testament and Ethics, but essentially I'm a friend of Patrice's who wonders how he shall survive her death. We argued about everything from the historical Jesus to the celibacy of the clergy in the Middle Ages. But I'm quite well-behaved really, and can be counted on to discuss other subjects. Did I notice you eyeing our lake with a view to a walk? May I join you?"

Kate, after regarding him for a moment, nodded, and they set off together. "As you have no doubt guessed," he said, "I have lain in wait for you. I decided you could do worse than to hear first from me in the matter of Patrice. If you neither like nor believe me, well, that would be true anytime we met. You mentioned Veronica. There will be Veronica, and many others, most of them women. The men did not take to Patrice, as a whole, at least not those as long in the

45

tooth as she and I; nor did the established women, for the most part. Classics, particularly, deeply resented her views of the goddesses, Artemis, Athena, and of personalities like Antigone. Classicists are a particularly insular bunch who expelled Nietzche, loath the Cambridge school—Frazer, Murray, Cornford, especially Jane Harrison—and spend the greater part of their energies trying to stamp out comments on the classics made by those not properly initiated into the language. They are rather like priests before the Reformation. It seemed best that you hear me first. Would you like to circle the lake moving to your right or left?"

"Which way did Patrice go?"

"With me? Right, always."

"But the conversation went left?"

"In the eyes of many, yes. What you'd better understand from the first," he continued, as they set out at a brisk pace to the right, "is that I loved Patrice. There is no other word to explain what I felt for her. I'm married, and my wife loved her also. One did love her, if one cared for her at all. She was not a person about whom one felt tepid emotions. If she loved you, you loved her and continued to, even when months went by without a meeting. We have experienced much of what there is to experience together. Toward the end, though I didn't know it was the end, I held her in my arms and tried to give her courage."

"Was she depressed, or afraid?"

"Oh, yes. She was often that. You do not ask if we were ever lovers?"

"It didn't seem important. I assume it wasn't the basis of your relationship?"

"Of course it wasn't. We were young together. We grew old. Our children became adults. But what was between us never really changed, though we each changed so much: Patrice had a mystical streak, the sort of thing, I mean, that made her write so wonderful a book about witches, and I am a rather ponderous expounder of theology, and these were always true of us.

All that changed was our relation to the world; Patrice became famous, and I became, at least on this campus, notorious. My views on Christ are considered quite renegade, I assure you."

"I've heard," Kate mused, walking along at his side, and understanding why Patrice must have found comfort in his tweed jacket and broad chest, "that they used to throw women suspected of being witches into lakes: if they sank, they were innocent, if they floated, they were guilty and therefore condemned to death. Maggie Tulliver thought that rather unfair and so do I. I know little or nothing about Patrice, really, but I imagine she was rather like Maggie as a girl. George Eliot, you know, *The Mill on the Floss.* She drowned at the end, being a witch. Was Patrice a witch, do you think?"

"What a very interesting woman you are," Bertie said. "I never thought of that."

"What was Patrice working on at the end? Not ready to publish, I don't mean, but brooding about, writing drafts of each day?"

"Middle age, would by my guess. And death. It was what she talked of, when she was talking to those she trusted." Kate nodded. "I think she was very excited about it, whatever it was. I don't believe she would have taken her life before she had finished it. That's what makes me convinced on the subject. Oh yes, I might say, she believed that one should not wait around to be invaded by old age. She believed in ending it at the chosen moment. But I don't think this was the chosen moment. Not very persuasive, is it?"

"That worries her biographers," Kate said. "Tell me about her. I wish I knew what I wanted to ask. What did she look like, for example, what was her physical presence like?"

"I thought you'd met her."

"I did meet her, once. I'm not very good at looks, I'm afraid. I remember her as someone whose dress and demeanor said to me, instantly, she's concerned with things that have nothing to do with wealth, or style, or fashion. Her hair looked as though she had trimmed it herself with a child's scissors. Her shoes announced that she intended to walk in them, that was what shoes are for. Everything about her spoke of someone who had got down to the essentials of life. And yet, she was traveling, she may have looked different at other times. Did she ever get herself up to be dashing, in a cap, perhaps, or a large hat?"

Bertie laughed. "Not in recent years. When she was young, it was all different. Lately, all she wanted was to live intensely, to avoid chitchat, not to waste time, though she would spend it lavishly where her imagination was caught. I remember once, at some faculty thing, she explained to the wife of some elderly professor that the students in her class had not believed her when she had described girdles and how all women used to wear them to assure their looking neat and unwobbly. The woman said, yes, she'd noticed a number of her friends didn't wear girdles and didn't seem to know that, with the weight and spread the years bring, they looked quite wobbly ungirdled. But, Patrice said, perhaps they don't care how they look? And then she turned away, because it was quite clear the woman had wholly missed the point. She hadn't much time for people like that. But if the smallest cleft opened to let in light, she would be as patient as only a gifted teacher can be, encouraging enlightenment. She honestly didn't give a damn what people thought, honestly didn't, and looked it. And of course, she was beautiful, in a certain way. Not, I might add, to make all things clear, in your way."

"Not."

"No. You are quite elegant, and slim, and were, obviously, born knowing how to look elegant without half trying. Patrice could be at home in a large, wooly sweater with a turtle neck, or, in earlier years, in some smartish dress she'd had the good luck to pick off a rack somewhere, but she was never elegant, and the ignorant might think her dowdy, as they could never you. My god, how hard it is to bring people to life. And yet I wish for five minutes you could turn into her, just to feel her presence.''

"What was it she made you feel, with her presence?''

"Well, excited by an idea, of course, or strengthened in your determination to buck the system, but chiefly, what she made you feel was that you had come home. Can you possibly know what I mean?''

"I suspect you have that effect yourself,'' Kate said. "When one knows you better, or speaks to you of one's profoundest doubts.''

"Perhaps. I learned it from her. Or perhaps, she from me. I know no modesty in speaking of what we had from one another. Through knowing her I became a better person, and she said the same of me. But what you must do, you know, is circulate around the campus and pick up all the chitchat you can about the two of us, alone or in tandem. We are not well thought of, on the whole.''

"Are there always this few people around the lake?''

"Oh, yes. It's a vigorous walk, and only undertaken by the determined and hardy, or the desperately lonely student. But students are discouraged; there have been rapes, I regret to say. We live in terrible times. Students are urged not to walk alone.''

"When I went to college,'' Kate said, "walking alone was all that kept me sane. How sad for the students. Talking to you now, I feel almost in Patrice's presence. But, I haven't a clue what I'm here for, apart from the beastly task force, nor what I'm to accomplish. It's almost as though I were planning to write her life, and I don't know where to begin.''

"And when you are finished, her biographers can begin. I've met them, of course. Worthy of Patrice, I think. If only they can get on with it.''

"I expect I better start right off with some people who disliked her. Have you a practical suggestion?''

"More than that, I've taken steps. We, my wife and

49

I, are giving a sherry party this evening. We've invited representatives of both classics and English, not to mention history."

"But why should they come if they dislike you?"

"My dear, at a women's college in a small town, you all visit each other. There's nothing else to do. Where else can people stand in corners and connive and gossip? And your reputation has preceded you, by the way. I promise you something besides sherry. What shall it be?"

"Straight gin, I should think," Kate said, grinning at him, and taking his arm over a rough place.

"You are wondering," he said, "if Patrice liked or even tolerated cocktail parties. Well, she didn't. It was one of the things we didn't agree on. I like parties where there are people one can talk to, either to pick up news and opinions, or to hear their outrageous views on many topics; often, of course, one accomplishes both. Patrice hated the superficiality of the conversations, and more than that, I think, the pecking order such parties always encourage. One has to decide if the person one is talking to is worth talking to by all sorts of criteria Patrice liked to avoid, when possible. And, looking as she did, and given the status of aging women in our society, she always found that no one sought her out until they knew who she was, a policy she scorned. Where do you stand in this endless debate?"

"Oh, I hate parties for myself," Kate said, "but when sleuthing I find them invaluable. One doesn't need a reason for asking direct and outrageous questions, which are my favorite kind. Such as: I'm here on the task force; what do you, dear Professor of Classics, think of Gender Studies? If I went to ask them in their office, they'd be all official and give me a measured view. Standing with a drink in one hand, they'll tell me exactly what they think, and all about themselves in the bargain."

"Good," he said. "Come at five-thirty. I'll try to drop in on your conversations from time to time, and

50

annoy my collegues into revealing their fears, hang-ups, and narrow opinions.''

Bertie had, indeed, provided gin, as well as sherry, white wine, and soft drinks for the abstemious. His wife turned out, not to Kate's surprise, to be the sort of woman described as feminine. That is, though she might pursue a career and was, in fact, doing so, one could never imagine her—how did Kate want to put it? Yes, that was it: in a girls' school play, she would never be cast in a male role. Her name was Lucy, and she sipped sherry as one to the manner born; Kate, born to the same manner, would have actually drunk plain soda water over sherry: it was classed by her, most unfairly she had repeatedly been told, with sweet wine, and nothing could induce her to consume it. It had, of course, been her mother's favorite, indeed only, alcoholic beverage. Lucy might like sherry, but she had also liked Patrice.

"I'm glad you've come to Clare," Lucy said. "Bertie and others not only miss Patrice, not only mourn her, but they feel like Antigone: you know, as though she were unburied, like the brother I mean, not Antigone, though she was buried too, wasn't she?''

"What a good metaphor," Kate said, disentangling the Greek drama with no trouble. "I do think you've actually described what we are all, in our various ways, after. Tell me how you thought of her." But before Lucy could do so, the guests had begun to arrive in numbers.

At first, as was to be expected, everyone, having been introduced to Kate, confined themselves to seemly questions and remarks. But Kate soon identified a professor of classics and her husband who together formed a pair particularly scornful of Patrice in life and death, and she approached them quite boldly. Kate guessed that a reference to gender studies—a subject on which, in fact, she had no educated views, though she had been rather hoping to acquire some

51

from the task force—would simply evoke a potted lecture on the ignorance of feminists when dealing with the classics. Kate was far too impatient by nature to listen to lectures so familiar she could have delivered them herself, an impatience, Reed insisted, that explained her extreme partiality for the plays of Tom Stoppard. "I often wonder," Kate therefore said, "why no women's college has been named after Athena?"

"Thank god it hasn't," the classics professor snorted. "Not but that Athena hasn't been president of one; I always imagine that M. Carey Thomas was the modern incarnation of Athena, from which may we be preserved."

"Full of wisdom, you mean, and justice?"

"Unfeminine, imitating men, and devoid of wifely virtues."

"How interesting," Kate said. "Do you feel all college presidents should be wives?"

"I wouldn't go that far; but they ought at least not to get themselves up to look as though a hike were imminent."

"Like Patrice Umphelby, you mean?"

"Oh, did you know Patrice? You must have, to have picked so good an example. Though Patrice was never president of a college, for which heaven may be duly praised."

"Were you troubled by her death?"

"Of course I was, we all were. Troubling the college was perceived by Patrice to be her destiny in life, and she apparently embraced it as her destiny in death. Virginia Woolf and Sylvia Plath are two women writers I cannot abide, but at least they had the grace to kill themselves in a river or their own home. The lot of them, if you ask me, were simply like too many women today: self-indulgent, self-pitying, refusing to consider anyone but themselves."

"Perhaps, like the Amazons, they considered other women?"

"There were no Amazons," the professor answered, with a sneer that must, Kate thought, have been audible on the other side of the lake. "The Greeks thought women the scum of the earth, dogs at least, and the equal of slaves, and to romanticize their view of women is to deny all the historical evidence. Most of it, of course, available only in Greek."

"Would you say that the college feels now about Patrice rather as Antigone felt about her brother whose body had been left unburied? Lucy suggested that, and I thought it rather well put."

"Lucy knows nothing about it, charming woman though she is. Antigone, in fact, was a pig-headed fool, and so the Greeks perceived her. The rot I have had to listen to and read about Antigone!"

"How trying," Kate said.

"It all comes from reading Greek plays in translation, and thinking you know anything about them. And what feminists do with Greek texts. One despairs."

"Difficult for you," Kate said. "Are you a classicist too?" Kate asked the husband, who rather to her surprise was still attending to this conversation.

"Yes, I am," he said. "But retired now, you know. I had the good fortune to leave the profession before the current waves of nonsense quite overwhelmed us."

"Too early for the feminists," Kate said, "too late for Nietzsche, what good timing." The male classicist looked at Kate as though uncertain whether to attribute her remark to gin, sarcasm, or plain good sense. But in a manner peculiar to parties, the three of them slid apart and took care, for the rest of the evening, not to let their eyes meet.

Since Bertie had invited members of those departments least likely to have been supportive of Patrice and her aims while she lived, or to mourn her after death, Kate did not hear much in her favor. She had been dead long enough to have passed the border line before which one's reputation is allowed to be unassaulted: *nisi bonum,* and all that. What soon became clear to Kate was that Patrice had become, on the campus, a center of dissenting opinion, particularly as it concerned the teaching of history, English literature, and classics; her age and position had offered courage and support to those who questioned the intellectual positions of safe and, in the opinion of many, moribund disciplines.

"This," said Bertie, joining Kate with a man safely in tow, "is Professor Fiorelli. He led the fight to admit men to Clare College and doesn't see why women would want to isolate themselves in college when they live with men afterward. I thought," Bertie said, turning to Professor Fiorelli, "that you might try your arguments on Professor Fansler."

"You will scarcely need arguments," Kate said. "I don't know what I think about single-sex colleges. After all, the picture has certainly changed now that there are no all-men's colleges."

"My point exactly," Professor Fiorelli said, all but pounding her on the back. "Good to have a sensible woman around here for a change. We came damn close to getting men, and would have, probably, if Patrice Umphelby hadn't used her considerable charms, which were absolutely invisible to me by the way, to swing the balance."

"But surely one person couldn't make that much difference in an issue of that dimension."

"That's what you think. She firmed up the opposition. And a bunch of ladies-luncheon types they were; they needed firming up."

"I'm surprised you teach in a woman's college, if your opinion of women is so low. Surely there would be more prestige elsewhere, where you were not confined to only female students."

"I'd prefer it, of course, but it isn't that easy to move around these days. And there are a lot of advantages to teaching here. Just take the athletic facilities. When the girls are gone, we can use everything, the golf course, the tennis courts, the recreation building, the lake; and it's a nice town to bring up children in. But one does, from time to time, wonder a little about one's manhood. I hear you're on the Gender Studies task force, and I do hope you are going to be sensible about that, Professor Fansler. Teaching in a women's college is all right, but in a women's college with Gender Studies—I might turn into a eunuch. To be frank, Professor Fansler,'' and Professor Fiorelli lowered his voice, ''I don't think women who want to study women *like* men; they want to turn their backs on all Western literature, and turn each other on instead, ha, ha.''

Kate looked at him so long and steadily that he became uncomfortable. ''Are you,'' he asked, ''er, married?''

''Are you?'' Kated asked, she hoped sweetly.

It began to dawn on Professor Fiorelli that he had not, perhaps, picked the right recipient for his views. It was so hard to tell these days, even attractive women, if aging . . . Kate could read his thoughts as though they had been flashed on a prompt screen.

''Would you say,'' Kate asked him with genuine interest in his answer, ''that men who have studied only men all these years didn't like women?'' But Kate decided she did not need to wait for his answer. She had, moreover, a terrible feeling that this was the first of many such conversations. Such conversations, she had begun to notice years ago, always threatened to form established patterns, like soldiers on parade.

''There's another point,'' he said. ''If we start putting one woman author in each course, she'll be a token woman. They don't want that, do they? Or second-rate writers just because they're women?''

''I never before really noticed,'' Kate said, ''how many second-rate men we tolerate only because they're men. Do you think perhaps we ought to give our attention to what interests us? Not that I don't sympathize with your problem,'' she hastened to add, before he could ask her if they were still talking about literature.

"I teach nineteenth-century English literature, and there is no question about women authors there. The important question there is, shall we make room for Trollope?"

"Well," he said, "welcome aboard. Let me know if there's anything, anything at all. And have a happy."

"No," a voice behind Kate said, "you didn't miss anything. That's how he talks when he's not thinking. Better, in my opinion, than when he is thinking. He would, I ought in honesty to report, return the compliment. Geddes is my name, professor of psychology, friend and admirer of the late, sorely missed, Patrice. Bertie thought you might need rescuing. I was invited for just such squadlike activities. Would you, perhaps, like a little air? There's a nice backyard, as we used to call it when I was a boy."

"I would," Kate said, "love air above all else. How clever of you to have guessed."

"Did you know Patrice?" Geddes asked when they were outside in what could scarcely have been called a backyard anywhere, at any time.

"Ours," Kate said, "was a theological relationship exclusively. Professor Fiorelli would no doubt have recommended a convent. How well did you know her?"

"We were likely to become good friends when she died. We had discovered that we were interested in many of the same things. It is a kind of miracle to find a new friend in a college like this where you have spent so many years, and fall into so many routine relationships. I feel intensely deprived."

"Am I to understand," Kate said, "that unlike Professor Fiorelli, you do not feel emasculated because you teach women?"

"I did at one time, at least to a degree. I would be lying if I didn't admit to having dreamed of a great university where the important things happened. And then I became very interested in my work, I got an important grant for a longitudinal study, and I think I

56

have done something important. That does, you know, make all the difference.''

"What are you studying?'' Kate asked. ''Or is that the sort of question that is unanswerable in the length of time devoted to a new acquaintanceship undertaken at a cocktail party?''

"Of course it is. But in another way, it's simple enough to state. I'm studying various stages in people's lives, and the satisfaction they derive at various stages. What we must do, you see, is stop assuming attitudes, such as that all widows are unhappy, and actually discover what people feel. Naturally, since the study concerns women as well as men and was rather revolutionary in its findings Patrice was interested. There was even talk of her writing an introduction to the book. But that, alas, is not to be.''

"Shall we go in?'' Kate asked. ''I want to ask endless questions, of course, but think perhaps I had better seize this social chance to meet a few more members of the faculty, delightful and challenging as they all are.''

"Well, I'm glad that Bertie was able to provide you, in my humble self, with at least one person who admired Patrice this side of idolatry. She was, on the whole, I fear, rather looked at askance.''

"And,'' Kate said, ''they're all secretly grateful that she has removed herself from the scene.'' She led the way inside. ''What's more,'' she added, ''I suspect that they think the deity in which they believe and whose commandments they embody probably saw to it.''

"No doubt,'' Geddes said. ''Shall I get you another drink before you beard the English department?''

"How thoughtful,'' Kate said. ''Gin, I think. Straight.''

But before she had even reached for the drink, Bertie walked up to her. ''So there you are,'' he said. ''I thought the night had swallowed you. Someone's been trying to get you on the phone. Will you call him back, he said. Tell her, he said, it's the biographer.''

Chapter 6

No pleasure could equal, she thought . . . this having done
with the triumphs of youth, lost herself in the process of
living, to find it, with a shock of delight, as the sun rose, as
the day sank.
VIRGINIA WOOLF

*K*ate walked back to the alumnae house, glad to
escape the rest of the party and especially the English
department, at least for the present. She placed her call
from her room and waited to hear from Archer or Herbert. It intrigued her to observe how stimulated she was
at the thought of talking to them. They are New York,
she thought; not this rural paradise surrounding a lake,
where everyone fears change.

It was Archer. Herbert, he said, after barely greeting
her, was worried. He had talked with the children,
well, actually, with one of the children, the daughter,
the oldest. Could Kate come back to New York City
where she belonged, and confer?

"AT&T has," Kate pointed out, "provided us with
the means of speaking across distance. Do you, in the
throes of your Humpty Dumpty complex, again suspect eavesdroppers?"

"I want you to hold my hand and murmur comfort-

58

ing things. So does Herbert. Have you decided to adopt the life of the single-sex, rural college?''

"What an idea! I did, however, agree to serve on a task force, and it has its first meeting tomorrow. Can you wait? You could always take the shuttle up here, you know. But if it's that urgent . . ."

"I shall meet you at the airport when you return tomorrow and explain all. What shuttle are you taking? The two o'clock? The only thing is, if you can find a moment tomorrow, or better still tonight, you might just have a few minutes' chat with Veronica Manfred. Professor of comparative literature, I think.''

"Tenured, I assume," Kate said.

"I always thought so, but don't ask me to explain the finer points of academic advancement at Clare. Perhaps, before boarding the nasty little shuttle, you could have a word with her, garner an impression, see if she is at all forthcoming, fills you with ideas.''

"Forthcoming about what?" Kate said. "Archer, I'm becoming worried. You're fine, aren't you, my dear?''

"Herbert and I are worried to death, and extremely unhappy. Also we miss and need you. I shall be at the Eastern terminal when the shuttle lands, and shall talk your ear off all the way back to Manhattan. Since you are arriving in the rush hour, no doubt we shall be stuck in traffic on that dreary highway, and I shall have time to tell you all about everything. Till then, dear Kate.''

Kate hung up the phone, lost in puzzlement. Still, Archer had said to see Veronica, and she had no choice but to try. Kate had developed great faith in Archer. She looked at her watch to see that it was not yet nine o'clock. The room in which she sat, being owned by the college, boasted a directory of the community. Kate looked up Manfred and, before thinking too much, dialed the number. The phone was answered by a woman who, to Kate's great relief, announced herself. "Veronica Manfred here," the voice said.

"Ah," Kate answered, "Kate Fansler here. I don't know if you know who I am."

"A modest question that ill becomes your reputation as a scholar and detective," Veronica Manfred said. "Have you eaten?"

"As a matter of fact, no," Kate said, rather to her own astonishment. "Have you?"

"No. I was planning to swoop down upon Bertie's cocktail party at nine and gather you up. No doubt you have been warned that I would do just some such thing. Or do you practice telepathy?"

"Sometimes I wonder," Kate said. "I'm in the alumnae house. Can we eat here?"

"Certainly not. They stop serving at eight, and, anyway, if we are going to advertise our conversation, we might as well talk into an amplifying system and be done with it. Let's eat here. I've a casserole and the makings of a salad. I'll pick you up. Can you be downstairs in ten minutes? I've only scotch, gin, and wine, by the way. Will that do?"

"Actually," Kate said, "I'm considering giving up drinking. I seem to have acquired a reputation for thinking of nothing else."

"Well, don't start tonight is my advice. I'm even determined to put up with your notorious smoking."

"I shall try to be properly grateful," Kate said. "Gin will be fine. It seems to have become my drink at Clare College. See you in ten minutes."

Veronica lived in what e. e. cummings would have called a "pretty how" apartment. Kate's views of apartments were not dissimilar to her views on restaurants. Decoration bored her, particularly if the hand of a decorator were even infinitesimally discernible. On the other hand, she admired space, comfortable chairs, and the sense of someone living there, above all working there, rather than the sense which she got from too many living rooms in New York, which, to Kate's eye, sat up and said: haven't I been well planned and well furnished, aren't I original and tasteful? Veronica's living room showed no sign of sitting up and saying anything except: someone works here; sit down and converse.

Veronica supplied the gin and, with a certain grimace, an ashtray. "It's about Patrice, of course. You will have guessed that. Perhaps Archer and Herbert haven't mentioned me. I frighten them a bit, I think, and they are, so to speak, keeping me on ice."

"Well," Kate said, "you are off the ice. They may in fact have mentioned you, in all our talk about Patrice."

"It doesn't matter. I think they suspect that I was in love with Patrice, and in a way they are right, I suppose, though not in the way they think. I loved Patrice as I have loved only one other person, my mother. Yet you see, it is men who excite me, men whom I dream of. I have dreamed of them so long, lived in imagination their ranging lives, understood so well their lusts, that I have seen no reason to love one of them. I am a virgin, nearing fifty, and fiercely proud of it."

"And you are telling me this," Kate said, "daring me to decide you are a kook, some sort of nut, daring me to brush you off so you will not have to tell me what you have made up your mind to tell me, but rather hope to be let off from telling. Go on, *épatez moi*, though I doubt your little game will succeed."

"They said you were clever, Archer and Herbert. What do you think of them, by the way? I have known Archer for years, and loved him it goes without saying—not the way I loved Patrice, or my mother— lusted for him, I mean. But he doesn't care for women, not sexually. I appear always to have lusted after unavailable men; only lately have I come to realize that that was so, just as only lately have I found pride in my virginity, the fact that I am whole and untouched."

"To the Greeks, of course," Kate said, "virginity

61

meant that one was one's own person, not just without sexual experience.''

"So I have heard. But certain men know what I mean also. It is not considered a defensible position, but it is a real one, at least in our world, and perhaps even, like Artemis, for certain Greek women. I don't care for Herbert. Do you know why? His clothes. Herbert will make possible the writing of Patrice's life, so I tolerate him; Archer needs Herbert. But I detest the way his trousers hang on him like clothes from some larger person, thrown to him by a rescuer. I like men's clothes to fit them closely. I like the crotch smoothly, mysteriously, to suggest what it covers. Do I strike you as a typical virgin? I am also an editor of English Renaissance manuscripts and a specialist in Renaissance music.''

"Yes," Kate said, "I know. At least, I know about the music bit. Your work is well known. What I cannot understand is whether you have chosen me to discuss men's trousers with because I am likely to be horrified, or whether it is a vein of conversation you have lately taken up for the hell of it.''

"Archer said you were special. I guess he was right. I take it you never met Patrice, professionally, I mean, apart from that time in the airport. Archer mentioned that too.''

"No.''

"Yet she has stirred your imagination. 'Women alone stir my imagination,' she said to me, soon after we had met. It turned out to be a quote from Virginia Woolf. I knew instantly what she meant. One of the aspects of men which makes lusting after them so easy is that one always knows them; they are so rarely if ever mysterious, though some of them, the exceptional ones, are kind or devoted. But women can surprise you. I think that's what she meant.''

"You are proving the point nicely," Kate said. "Sorry, but you have certainly stirred my imagination. And yet, you know, George Eliot said that she didn't particularly like women. I think that was because a hundred years ago, she could imagine no surprises available to them, whereas men could suddenly believe in Darwin or leave their wives for the right reasons.''

"There is a great deal I would like to tell you about Patrice," Veronica said, as though this chitchat had gone on long enough. (My god, what chitchat, Kate thought.) "If I don't tell you, no one will ever know it, because we didn't write to one another. We always talked, here at the college. Have biographers really thought of that—how they prize documents, but that the important exchanges in a life are not documented because they are conveyed *viva voce*. In marriages we only know what the two said to one another if they were often apart and corresponded; we never know what they said alone together, if anything. The same is true of friendships, except that we can assume they said something, or would not have continued friends.''

"I can't decide whether you are more dubious about marriage or biography.''

"Equally, I think. They both are simply scripts someone has decided to make public. They bear little relation to the truth, whatever that is. But to return to Patrice. After her marriage ended, when her husband was murdered in New York, knocked down by thugs and shot, she became a different person. But in a sense she had always been that person; the new Patrice was simply waiting, or at any rate, ready, to step forth as her new self. She had, for example, to adjust herself to living alone; yet in a way she, like most women in marriages, had always lived alone.''

"Had you ever thought of living with her, hoped perhaps?'' Kate asked.

Veronica regarded Kate with an expression which could have turned, on the instant, to disdain or tolerance. Kate watched with a certain disinterest. She had long observed that plenty of people could question; few could bear to be questioned in turn in quite so probing a way. But Veronica's face indicated tolerance. "It's true, you have the right to ask questions like that. The answer is that we never came to it; Patrice and I both saw the dilemma: how when you live with people you open the greatest possible opportunity for irritation and smallest possible opportunity either for solitude or the intensity of real conversation. It seems better to pay the price for solitude and seek fine intensities away from the hearth. Since you are married, you might not mind saying whether or not you agree. Or do you take marriage to be fundamentally different than two unmarried people's sharing of an establishment?''

"Not a bit," Kate said. "If I am as frank as you, and that seems to be my destiny, I would say that I agree entirely, except where there are enough rooms, enough bathrooms, in short, enough space. I don't believe any relationship can succeed that doesn't offer both partners solitude and independence as a matter of course."

"That's a relief anyway. Do you read the *New York Times* on Sundays?"

"God willing."

"The magazine section some time back had a man on the cover, a cosmologist from Cambridge, England, with a motor-neuron disease who could hardly move or speak, but who could think, and who therefore was able to devote all his time to thinking about black holes and other such outer space subjects. I thought of Patrice instantly when I read about him, though you probably won't understand why. I mean, the author of the article said that the face of illness masked this man, Hawkins, Hawking, something like that, from the outsider: one saw only a paralyzed man in a wheelchair, and didn't see beyond it. Patrice was like that. After her husband's death, she just got down to fundamentals: just lived, and thought, mainly. But those who saw her saw only an aging woman, someone invisible in our society. She lived with the same intensity he lived with, that cosmologist, and no one wasted her time asking her to be a 'woman,' as no one wasted his time asking him to mow the lawn." Veronica paused a moment. "Yet, you know, there was still the difference between them. He had a wife and other women who saw to all his needs. He had female assistants and male students and peers. It doesn't work that way for a woman, of course. Still, Patrice didn't need that much help. No one asked her to serve them, even if they didn't serve her. Except her students, of course."

"What do you mean by got down to fundamentals?" Kate asked.

"You know, that wonderful freedom of the old, who don't give a damn. I once went to see a play by Jean Kerr. There was a young woman in it who had gone to the hairdressers for the first time in a while, and she reports in the play, and the line got a big laugh, that the hairdresser said to her, one more week and it would have been too late, as though she had cancer. Not having your hair done was like having a death dealing disease; I guess it is for most women. Patrice had escaped from all that."

"You dress with style," Kate observed. "Your own, but style."

"Yes. And for years I used to ponder Patrice's security in not bothering. And I used to wonder about the place where she found herself, and found that it was her self. But never mind all that. That isn't what I wanted to talk to you about. Not primarily. I wanted to talk about Patrice's death. As I believe, her murder."

"I've heard about your belief," Kate said. "You seem to have disturbed the campus all the way up to the president."

"Anything disturbs her which might upset her board of trustees and the ladies from the Clare College clubs in Iowa."

"Why Iowa?" Kate asked.

"Emblematic. They marry and join the local Clare College club because it reminds them of when they were in college and had slightly unusual ambitions, when they each imagined life might hold something different. Anyway, they give money, and not frightening

65

them is the first job of the president, or so she sees it. But I say, colleges of whatever sex must be devoted to the truth. And the truth is that Patrice would not have taken her own life, not then, and not in that way.''

''Do you say that because you knew her so well, or have you any more tangible evidence?''

''Plenty of tangible evidence. For one thing, she would have prepared me in some way, left a note. She couldn't have been that unkind. For another, the note she did leave. Preposterous. Charlotte Perkins Gilman indeed.''

''Meaning?''

''Meaning that Charlotte Perkins Gilman didn't kill herself just because life had got tiresome. She had cancer and decided to die when the cancer became too painful. Better chloroform than cancer, she said. The police had such trouble finding out who she was, they didn't go into the matter any further. Here's Charlotte Perkins Gilman's suicide message; see for yourself.'' She went to a desk and found a piece of paper which she handed to Kate. ''I was going to send it to you anyway.'' Kate took the paper, and read Charlotte Perkins Gilman's final note:

A last duty. Human life consists in mutual service. No grief, no pain, no misfortune, or ''broken heart'' is excuse for cutting off one's life while any power of service remains. But when all usefulness is over, when one is assured of an imminent and unavoidable death, it is the simplest of human rights to choose a quick and easy death in place of a slow and horrible one. Public opinion is changing on this subject. The time is approaching when we shall consider it abhorrent to our civilization to allow a human being to lie in prolonged agony which we should mercifully end in any other creature. Believing this choice to be of social service in promoting wider views on this question, I have preferred chloroform to cancer.

* * *

"You will notice," Veronica said, "that there is more than one inconsistency here. Patrice didn't have cancer, and didn't use chloroform. And would she, if she were killing herself, leave a note only to her children? And such a note? No, that note was written by someone else, typed, you will have noticed, but then Patrice always typed. It was written by someone who knew her well, but Patrice didn't write it. Whoever killed her wrote it."

"But why mention Charlotte Perkins Gilman at all?"

"It must have seemed so beautifully characteristic. Feminist to the end, don't you know, quoting another woman. But Patrice would have found her own words, I assure you of that."

And, more worried than convinced, Kate took herself off a few minutes later and so, wearily, to bed.

The task force, when it assembled the next morning, promised to offer farce in place of tragedy. The president turned up to greet them all, and then departed, leaving the group, whose task, Kate could not help but think, was uncertain and whose force minimal, to discuss why on earth a women's college should require gender studies. Those certain it should not had all their arguments marshaled and in order. Kate soon knew them all, and had to admire their cogency and respect their arguments. The arguments on the other side were sadly in arrears. The reason, Kate suspected, was that those chosen to represent it lacked either faith or knowledge. The task force had certainly been stacked. Kate marveled, not for the first time, at the ease with which academics deserted the cause of scholarly disinterest when their own most cherished opinions were at stake. The classicist of last night was present, and her condemnation of gender studies was clear, unemotional, and devastating. On the other side were ranged a dean, indifferent to the argument but nervous about anything that would affect admissions, and an aging female professor of psychology who, altogether uncertain of her own opinion, had been coached, as she all but admitted, by Professor Geddes. Kate said nothing, but promised herself to know more about this subject by the next meeting. Patrice, Kate said to herself, would you have been here? How much difference will your death make to this women's college? And she realized that for the first time, she was genuinely questioning that nighttime swim in the lake with pockets filled with stones.

The task force had been offered lunch in the alumnae house, but Kate skipped that in order to pack and get off. She had promised Archer to be on the two o'clock shuttle. As she came down with her suitcase to check out, she was told that Professor Geddes was on the phone for her. Kate spoke to him from the desk.

"Sorry to hear you're going so soon," he said. "I'd hoped to lure you to my home for lunch. We have one of the lovely faculty houses on the lake. Patrice liked to visit us here. Are you sure you couldn't take a later plane? If only spring were here, you could refresh yourself with a swim."

"In the lake?" Kate asked.

"Heavens, no. No one swims in the lake. In our pool. But we'll have to take a rain check."

"No doubt the task force will still be meeting then."

"I consider that a promise," he said. And Kate, hanging up the phone, bid the woman at the desk farewell and walked out to the car hired to take her to the airport.

"Not staying for lunch?" the classicist, passing Kate on her way to the dining room, asked. "We might talk about what we do know about the Greeks, and not Antigone," she added, in what she no doubt took to be a gracious tone.

"Soon, I hope," Kate said, not altogether insincerely. She was beginning to think that this pleasant rural college had a lot of explaining to do. I have not yet, Kate thought, met anyone here who is happy, at least no woman. Professor Fiorelli is happy in his mindless way, and Professor Geddes seems happy. Even Bertie is all right, apart from missing Patrice. But every woman I've met, from the president on down seems tense, or angry, or upset. How much is there to be said for women's colleges after all? And speeding away from the campus and toward, in the fullness of time, the Callahan Tunnel, Kate thought that next time she came she would have to have a much longer talk with Madeline Huntley.

Chapter 7

*Few women, I fear, have had such reason as I have to think
the long, sad years of youth were worth living for the
sake of middle age.*

GEORGE ELIOT

*W*hen Kate emerged from the shuttle, Reed,
not Archer, was waiting for her. Her heart leapt at the
sight of him—yes, she thought, it did leap, it is not just
a tired way of describing what happened—first at the
joy of seeing him unexpectedly, of meeting after separation, and then fear that something was wrong. But
with him standing before her, what could be wrong?
"Are you fine, then?" she said.

"Perfect." He took her arm and drew her toward
him, reaching at the same time for her suitcase. They
were just not the generation that embraced actually,
rather than symbolically, in public. Were we young,
Kate thought, our bodies would have touched and excited one another. As it is, we promise only with our
eyes: a matter of custom. Public embraces offend me: a
matter of upbringing.

"Archer called to say he was meeting you, and I
said, let me. I need to talk to her; what better place than

a traffic jam, which, of course, we shall thrust ourselves into."

"We could, since it is you," Kate said, feeling his arm against her, "have a drink or dinner here."

"The bars will be as crowded as the highway, and less private. And one cannot really drink if one is to drive. No, into the parking lot. Did you check any baggage?"

"Never," Kate said. "Not if I'm going for under a week. The agony of it, the frustration, even if it does turn up on one's plane. What is it, Reed? Anything to be anxious about?"

"Not anxious. Just excited I hope. All about my mid-life crisis. Leaving the DA's office, all that. Archer's waiting for you at home, by the way. You're to call him when you arrive. I have to be off to a meeting this evening. Is everything all right in New England?"

"I don't know that I'd say it's all right. Shall I drive, so that you can keep your mind on your story?"

"Good," he said, "if you're not too tired."

Kate started the car, thinking, How can I be this fortunate? How is it possible? And what will the gods say if they hear me? Reed handed her the money for the parking fee, and when, having waited on line, they had paid it and exited to the highway, she smiled at him to begin.

"I'm thinking of becoming a professor, if they'll have me, and they are making noises as though they will. Have you ever imagined being married to a professor?"

"Often, in my murky past. At least, as often as I imagined being married, which was seldom. But I never thought for a moment that the man I married would be one. Look at that, no signal lights, and he dodges from lane to lane like a spawning salmon. Reed, what extraordinary news. What will you teach? The contemporary marriage, its problems, perspectives, and future? You are an expert, my love."

71

Reed laughed. "Close to that," he said. "Criminal Procedure. At the Columbia Law School."

"Oh to be a lawyer," Kate said, reaching toward him, and taking her attention from the road long enough to let a car sandwich itself in between her and the car ahead. "They tell you not to tailgate," she said, "speaking of criminal procedure, but if you don't you are cut off and forced to tailgate into the bargain. When I think of my poor graduate students in English, shuttled off to Arkansas to hold forth sadly on Foucault and Virginia Woolf, and lawyers just decide to teach at Columbia. Do they hire any lawyer who says I'm ready for a spot of teaching, chaps; will next year do?"

"There are qualifications, I'm afraid, such as having edited law review in one's distant past. But what I really have to offer is what they call high-level experience in trial and appeals work. As some character in one of Faulkner's drearier novels said, 'I've seen it all,' and I mean all, from the earliest investigation to the final appeal after conviction. I, my love, have been part of the whole criminal justice system, at least in New York, whereas the majority of law professors, like most English professors, aren't exactly famous for their practical experience. In many fields, that doesn't matter. But in crim pro, as it's known to its friends and relations, it's essential to understand how the real-life situation works. I mean, there's not much sense in talking to a class in crim pro abstractly about trials, if one hasn't come to understand the long hard way that ninety percent of the cases never come to trial, but end up being settled through plea-bargaining."

"Reed, I feel like one of those dismal wives of yesteryear who never had the least idea what their husbands did at the office."

"What nonsense. Do I carry on when you have to explain all those fine points of literature and academic politics? Without you, would I ever have known that Fiona Macleod and William Sharp were the same person?"

72

"What a memory you've got! But why isn't everyone teaching at law school who knows as much as you do, always supposing, which I doubt, that anyone else does?"

"I love you when you put on wifely airs. The sad point is that here is where law professors distinguish themselves rather sharply from you English types. Lawyers, at least the law review types, can make so much money in private practice that they aren't exactly beating down the doors for a chance to teach. In fact, it's mostly those of us who went into public interest law who do, us, and the chaps who've already made their millions, or who go right on making them while teaching."

"And all I can think of to say is something hideously selfish: will I still be able to get inside help when I need to know what the police are up to?"

"One still has friends. Though if my real hope is granted me, there may be minor problems."

"Your real hope? Not, don't tell me, to become the chief lawyer of Tanzania?"

"No, my love. To become a judge. On the Federal District Court, which is not altogether unlikely, or the New York Court of Appeals, which is wholly unlikely. As you see, I have developed hubris in my old age. My middle age, I should emphatically say, thinking of your Patrice. She gave me courage, she did. I want to hear about her and Clare."

"Not before you explain about judges. Do you just apply for the job, and why not the Supreme Court of New York? Only the highest court for my man."

"Because it isn't the highest court, not in New York which for reasons lost in the past, calls its lowest court supreme, and its highest, to which I long to attain, the court of appeals."

"And how does one get to be a judge? Don't tell me it's by bribing the right people. I don't think you should have that much of a middle-age crisis."

"Some judges are elected, my dear, as you will remember if you recall the last time you voted. Some are appointed, by the governor, or the senator of the party in power. These, when enlightened, usually ask a panel to recommend some likely candidates. As I said, it's a long shot. But I don't think our Patrice would call a short shot the proper middle-age dream, do you?''

''And if one has taught for some years, one is more beautifully eligible?''

''One is. There are other routes, but for me that's the likeliest one. Also, one is interested in teaching. Also I'll get a chance to write some scholarly articles which will impress everyone.''

''For the Harvard Law Review, I suppose? No, don't tell me now. I want to digest all this. Later on, you must find me a course for spouses of lawyers, propounding all the ins and outs. In your case, of course, ins. So you are really more qualified to teach criminal procedure than I am to teach novels or the nineteenth century, neither of which I have created or experienced: a sobering thought. Reed, I am glad.''

He took the offered hand, after which she eased into the right-hand lane on the Triborough Bridge. Waiting in line to pay the toll, Kate chuckled. ''I took a Stevie Smith novel for my bedtime reading at Clare,'' she said, ''and I came across a wonderful passage. The central character happens to read in a newspaper about a divorce case that had not succeeded. The newspaper reported that 'the judge said that he sympathized with the plaintiff, but the inability to institute or to sustain a conversation was no grounds for divorce.' Good thing it isn't, from what I've heard; there would be damn few marriages. Ours among them, praise be.''

''Pull up then, and let me drive while you tell me about college life in New England.''

''I can do that while driving,'' Kate said. ''College life in New England depresses me. There is a classics professor, for example, who one can see would have drawn the very life from Patrice. Not that she isn't accomplished in her way, and I suppose in another time,

74

might even serve as a fairly adequate colleague. It is as Woolf's Mrs. Dalloway said of Miss Kilman: 'No doubt with another throw of the dice, had the black been uppermost and not the white, she would have loved Miss Kilman. But not in this world. No.' ''

"You do realize I haven't an idea what you're talking about. Almost home, anyway. Shall you have to call Archer right away?"

"I am sure," Kate said, stopping at a light, "that Archer expected us to be caught in a far worse traffic jam. We might have been hours."

In the end, when Reed had left for his meeting, Kate and Archer had dinner together. Herbert, poor dear, was teaching a night course. But Kate felt his presence, even though she was, thanks to Veronica, glad not to be forced to contemplate his trousers. Archer, as always, was impeccable from head to toe. The head looked troubled.

"We've found more things," he said darkly. "Another part of the journal, and something else very troublesome. The daughter came to see me. She'd like to meet you, by the way. Did you know you're the kind of person people hear mentioned and say, 'Oh, I'd love to meet her.' ''

"I didn't know that," Kate said. "But far better to be your sort, whom people meet and say: I'd like to know him, preferably forever. Veronica says she was in love with you."

"Veronica presents certain difficulties."

"All right, keep a gentlemanly discretion. And I shall be ladylike, and not probe. But she is convinced that Patrice did not take her own life. The question, obviously, is how objective is Veronica?"

"It's worse than that. Veronica actually sued Patrice once, claiming coauthorship of one of Patrice's books. We were bound to come upon it sooner or later, but it is amazing she never told me. It happened, of course, before I met Veronica, and isn't, I dare say, the sort of thing one brings up on a frivolous evening."

"What did she sue her for?" Kate asked.

"She said that she had helped Patrice with one of her books to the point of having written part of it; she wanted to be called a coauthor and to share in the profits."

"And you learned all this from the new part of the journal?"

"No. Oddly enough, I learned it from the daughter, who mentioned it rather casually when I said something about Veronica. The case was eventually settled. The daughter remembered Patrice saying at the time that what Veronica was really suing her for was alienation of affection."

"Veronica never breathed a word to me," Kate said. "She made it sound as though each of them had the other's well-being at her heart's core."

"So she wishes now, I dare say. The case is a fascinating one, which has introduced me to all the amazing permutations of copyright law. The things that go on everyday, that dazzlingly happen, and unless one's attention is drawn to them, one never notices. I called my lawyer, in one of those midtown firms, and she said . . ."

"Archer, the beauty of that 'she,' not even made a point of. No wonder every woman loves you, your charms aside."

"She said," (and that Archer did not elaborate in any way on her comment was pure Archer, she thought; how much the gift of conversation was letting certain things alone) "that the case had made a certain minor mark on copyright history, and recommended me to several weighty sources. You've no idea how complicated is the idea of copyright infringement, let alone authorship. There's a wonderful case involving Sherlock Holmes. But let us stick resolutely to the point. But what was it?"

"Come home," Kate said, "and I'll give you a

brandy. We must, of course, talk about Veronica. And the new-found part of the journal. You've brought it, I hope."

"You," Archer said, "will be suing us next for co-authorship of Patrice's biography."

"As someone said in quite other circumstances, not bloody likely. Shall we take a taxi, or walk?"

Swilling brandy in her balloon glass, an exercise she enjoyed rather more than the brandy itself if truth be told, Kate felt a strange contentment. My forensic day, she thought: Reed on his career in law, Archer on the law of authorship. "We ought, I know," she said, "to discuss Veronica, but I long to hear about the lawsuit. Not her motives, that is, but what she claimed. 'Why' can wait."

"I hope you are right. No question, chatting on infinitely anecdotally about copyright law turns out to be one of life's rare pleasures. Who would have guessed?" Archer, too, swilled his brandy in the glass, sniffing it occasionally in the best club man manner. "Well, my dear, prepare yourself to be fascinated. But it is necessary first to make the distinction between copyright infringement and claims of coauthorship. Are you sure you are quite ready?"

"Pretty sure," Kate said. "But it begins to sound like something one could get a firmer grasp on in the morning, like the latest critical theories."

"Not that bad. Example: *Sheldon* v. *MGM:* opinion by Judge Learned Hand reversing the opinion of the lower court. Had the movie about the Madeline Smith case, the Glasgow woman who did or did not poison her lover, infringed upon the copyright of someone who had written a play on that subject? Bear in mind that one cannot copyright a plot or an idea. Judge Hand said that copyright had not been infringed on. The facts were the facts, and several writers could well end up dramatizing them in a similar way. Second example: *The Seven Percent Solution*: Sherlock Holmes,

77

Freud, cocaine: good movie, good book. The idea of combining these three elements had first been set forth by a doctor in an article in a medical journal. The author of *The Seven Percent Solution* credited the article when he published his book. Doctor claimed he'd been infringed upon. Not at all, was the decision: you can't copyright an idea, let alone Sherlock Holmes or Freud. Do you begin to see the infinite joy in all this?''

"But," Kate said.

"No arguing. I'll send you copies of the relevant decisions or accounts of the decisions to be found in a book called *Plagiarism and Copyright* by a man named Lindley. He also tells the marvelous tale of *Rebecca*. You remember Rebecca, the beautiful and dangerous first wife?''

"Remember? It was the most absolutely compelling book I had ever read at that age. Did someone else claim to have written it?''

"Several people, my dear. And in a way they had. An old English home, a meek second wife, a handsome silent husband, an evil housekeeper—this is the very stuff of romance and the Gothic tale. But did they tell it as well as Daphne Du Maurier? No, they did not. And it is in the telling, more exactly in the writing down, the language, the ordering of events together with the way those events are expressed that constitutes authorship. The court found for Daphne, as well they might.''

"And they also found for Patrice?''

"In fact, Veronica's lawyer urged her to settle, which in the end she did. For more or less the same amount Patrice's lawyer had advised her to offer in the first place. And, needless to say, a fortune in lawyer's fees out of Patrice's pocket. A messy business, which seemed to attract very little attention at the time, I think because Patrice used the name Urghart rather than Umphelby for the trial. That was her maiden name. She had an affiliation with the letter U that one can only call purposeful: no one could have two such odd names beginning with the same letter by accident.''

"Archer, I haven't understood a thing, except about the letter U, which is, I feel confident, the only inessential point in your entire story. I have a genius for comprehending inessential points: they positively assault my mind and insist upon being comprehended, such as, what was Mary Queen of Scots' claim to the English throne?''

"Tell. I have always wanted to know.''

"Archer, behave. I want you to run Veronica's claims past me again, once more. Slowly. What sort of case did she really think she had?''

"I've already explained that, or Patrice's daughter has. She wanted Patrice to acknowledge her. She sued Patrice for alienation of affection.''

"Are you suggesting . . . ?''

"I never suggest, not about motives. But if you mean, do I think they were lovers or wanted to be, no. Life is more complicated than that. By the end of her life Patrice was open to many ideas she had, perhaps too readily, dismissed before. She wasn't one of those people, as you've already gathered, who simply become more so with age. That was what made her a miracle. But somehow, I think her body carried her to her adventures, I don't think it provided them.''

"Veronica said something like that,'' Kate said. "Something about a man at Cambridge University in a wheelchair, unable to move, who was somehow intensely free, therefore, to explore the universe. Can that be what she said? Perhaps I've inhaled too much brandy?''

"I know what she meant, oddly enough. I, too, thought of Patrice when I read that article. And yet, of course, she was nothing like that man: vigorous, she was, with long strides, and a way of throwing back her head and laughing. What were we talking about?''

"Why Veronica claimed coauthorship?''

"Oh, yes. Veronica had offered Patrice the idea, the

germ, so to speak, of her last novel. Not that Patrice denied it: the book contains, in fact, acknowledgment to Veronica, and thanks, all in the most proper and generous way."

"Henry James used to get germs all the time, at dinner parties—ideas for stories and novels I mean, not flu germs. And he always hated when people went on telling him more about the real life people than he wanted to know. None of the ladies who sat next to him ever claimed coauthorship, as far as I know."

"Exactly. But he, no doubt, cautious man, was careful not to see too much of them. Patrice saw rather a lot of Veronica, and may even have, more out of kindness toward Veronica than her own needs, but we shall never know, talked a bit about the book."

"Few authors do that," Kate said.

"But some show manuscripts to others. The guess of the daughter, and I agree with her, is that somehow Veronica felt the need, as Patrice started to draw away, to get her attention. Suing someone for coauthorship is one rather efficient way of doing it: I imagine it concentrates the mind on the suer with marvelous effect."

"But, Archer, why would Patrice offer to settle? Isn't that almost an admission of guilt, a way of saying that Veronica was right?"

"I'm sure Patrice felt that way. But in fact, it's so often cheaper to settle, and anyone who knows anything about it understands the situation. Patrice's lawyers, to their credit, urged her to make a substantial offer. But Veronica didn't want a settlement: she wanted attention."

"Like the sort of children who start fires in their rooms when their parents aren't treating them right."

"What extraordinary children you know. But the analogy is exactly right, I expect. Anyway, after endless work, delays, depositions, crowded court calendars—I do hope my expertise in this matter is impressing you with great force—the case came to court and there it was settled."

"And how did Veronica feel?"

"Aha. Madame Sherlock. How indeed? Can Patrice, saint though Herbert may believe her to be, have simply said: let us forgive and forget? She walked into that lake before telling anyone about it. Or if she did tell them, Herbert and I shall have to ferret it out. Could Veronica, one asks oneself, have had another threat up her sleeve?"

"The fact is," Kate said, "it's damn odd that Veronica never mentioned it to me, so buddy-buddy were we that night. Odder still is the fact that she insisted that Patrice had been murdered—would never, never have taken her own life then, in that way, with no message for Veronica. And then there's Charlotte Perkins Gilman."

"The woman mentioned in the suicide note?"

"She, it seems, had cancer. Patrice's note would have made sense only if she, Patrice, had had cancer, or some equally dread disease. That, at least, was Veronica's point."

"Which brings us," Archer said darkly, "to the part of the journal the daughter just found. It seems she may have."

"May have?" Kate said, feeling that they had fallen, suddenly, into a very Jamesian mode.

"May have had cancer."

"Shit," Kate said, in her most un-Jamesian manner. "Why do I suddenly feel a need for Herbert?"

"Herbert," Archer said, "is very upset. Like all of us, he is wracking his brain for explanations. I only pray they do not take a religious turn."

"Are you telling me that she indeed had the motive Gilman's final message suggested?" Kate asked, drinking the brandy rather quickly in a non-club man manner.

"Do you think we better have another drink?" Archer asked. "I might even take up smoking—it seems so satisfactorily to relieve one's tensions."

"That's because you have been watching movies,

either old ones made when everyone smoked, or new ones made by people in the pay of the tobacco companies. When I was growing up, it was almost impossible to make love without a cigarette, or rather two cigarettes. In fact, it was impossible to do anything at all. Did Patrice smoke?''

"She'd given it up. Often. Kate, my love, our biography is coming apart in our hands.''

"No it's not. Patrice is unchanged. If you understand her, and I suspect you do, you and Herbert, it will only get better. I think I hear Reed.''

"Might we mention this to him?''

"We might. I've never known it not to help. Archer, don't fret. Think what will become of us all, if you become less debonair, less altogether adorable. I feel it is your duty to keep up Herbert's spirits, and mine.''

"Wait,'' Archer said, rising to greet Reed, "until you have read the new part of the journal.''

"We,'' Kate said to Reed, "are about to have more brandy. Will you have a snifter?'' But rising to fill their glasses, she felt, for the first time since she had met Archer, afraid.

Chapter 8

*I have an intuition that I shall die in three years, so must
bustle about and do a lot of things in the time. When
do you expect to push off?*

ROSE MACAULAY

Kate crossed Park Avenue on her way to meet
Patrice's daughter, Dr. Sarah Umphelby. Archer had
moved, the evening before, from expostulation to per-
suasion in urging her to speak with Patrice's daughter.
"Is it," Kate had asked, "really my business?" The
brandy had made her not only wary but stubborn; furthermore, as she pointed out, with considerable vehemence and illustrative detail, she did not like doctors of
either sex or any specialty at any time.

Reed, who had the advantage of having arrived
newly on the scene, and consumed less brandy in the
course of the evening, had pointed out that this was intellectually indefensible as a position, and in the
cutting-off-one's-nose class enotionally speaking. Why
not find out what the woman wanted. "But," Kate had
asked, reasonably enough, "what can she possibly
want from me?"

Archer had been somewhat vague. "She and her
brother have chosen Herbert and me for the biography,

but she hardly chose us as partners in the investigation of her mother's death. Veronica, Clare College, the new section of the journal are all disturbing. I said that we had, even before the finding of the new journal section, consulted you, and she said, all right, she would talk to you, although," Archer had added with a certain emphasis, "she doesn't think much of amateur detectives, having taken a profound dislike to both Lord Peter Wimsey and Philip Marlowe at an impressionable age. I said there was little resemblance: you are taller than they and swagger less."

Kate, entering the building between Lexington and Park where the doctor daughter had her office, felt as unswaggering as possible. She had, she realized, identified, if that was the proper jargon, with Patrice. It was more than friendship you feel about her, feel you lost in not knowing her, Kate thought. Face it: she has become something more: who you might have been, or the mother you might have had. And now, you are to meet the daughter you might have had, and end up feeling deprived or grateful, as events reveal. Could one bear to meet a daughter who had not cherished such a mother? Yet how many daughters cherished their mothers? Well, quite a few, actually, particularly after the mother's death. But was it not easier to have a mother one despised and scorned, as she had hers, thinking always to oneself, This is what I do not want to be? Working-class mothers might provide their daughters with conflict: the daughters not wanting to be like their mothers, yet knowing their mothers were not to blame for being what they were. But with a mother such as mine, Kate thought, rich enough to have done anything, and stupid enough to have done nothing? What would it have been like to have had Patrice as a mother? What would it be like being Kate, to have an almost grown daughter?

Kate banished these nonproductive thoughts as she rang the bell and, following instructions, walked in.

The nurse or secretarty took her name and told her Dr. Umphelby was even now with her last patient of the day. Would Professor Fansler wait? Professor Fansler would, and, having hung up her coat, found herself, seated alone in the waiting room, as nervous as if she were going to be examined for a suspected fatal and debilitating disease.

And yet, when Sarah Umphelby appeared and invited Kate into her office, all the chimeras of the past hour dissolved themselves in the doctor's presence. She was a woman in her thirties, her hair well cut, her white coat almost hiding a full, tall figure. Thank god, Kate thought, I like her: she is neither officious nor arrogant. And I don't even know what kind of doctor she is. Kate asked.

"I'm an endocrinologist," she said. "All problems to do with the body's glands."

"What they called ductless glands when I was a girl," Kate said. "There was a time when glands were thought to be the secret of everything. Are they still?"

"If there are any 'secrets,'" the doctor smiled, "they are probably hidden in our immune systems. You remind me of my mother. She was fascinated by medicine and always used to get me talking about it, even when I was in medical school and bored every nonmedical person I knew to distraction. At first I wondered if it was tact, but she was clearly intrigued. And then, she was pleased to have a doctor daughter: it's the most emphatically nonhousewife thing one can do, and besides, she thought with a doctor in the family she'd find it easier to get prescriptions." Sarah smiled. "My brother did too. He was still in college when I began medical school, and he thought in three years I'd be able to get him all sorts of forbidden things. Fortunatley, he grew up."

"Where is he now?" Kate asked.

"In Washington. The state, I mean. He's a geologist, a specialist in volcanos. He's probably one of the

85

few people who found the eruption of Mt. St. Helens thoroughly satisfying.''

''Is he involved, I mean to the degree you are, in your mother's papers, the decision to have a biography, and so on?''

''Oh, yes. He was enormously fond of her, and, as a son, had far fewer problems with her than I did.''

''But,'' Kate said, ''I was just thinking as I came here, how wonderful to have a mother like Patrice. Or perhaps not wonderful—nothing to rebel against?''

''Something like that, I suspect. Oh, in the long run, we got along as well as any mother and daughter I know. But I do think that girls have special separation problems from their mothers, at least in our society where women do all the infant nurturing. And it is harder to separate from a good mother, in a way. Who'd be a parent?''

''So I have always thought,'' Kate said.

''I am one. But my husband spends more time with the baby than I do. One waits eagerly to see if this will make a difference. What I fear, of course, is that our daughter will, out of sheer perversity, take up bridge and join the Junior League.''

''Like my mother,'' Kate said, reviewing all her earlier thoughts. ''But no doubt she will find a new way to rebel. I met your mother once, did Archer tell you?''

''No. I suppose we had better talk about my mother. How is it, do you think, that happily concluded matters come undone so readily? First, we hadn't realized that my mother had left papers that would interest anyone. Then we were overwhelmed by people asking to see them and writing the greatest nonsense—when it wasn't simply boring. Then we found Archer and Herbert and seemed set for a biography when this new mess arose. The ridiculous idea that my mother didn't really commit suicide. And now, of course, we've found this new part of the journal.''

''Does it reveal something that changes everyone's ideas?'' Kate asked. ''Does she suggest that someone is trying to murder her and will probably succeed in making it look as though she drowned?''

"Nothing that dramatic. In fact, the new part of the journal is very much like the old one, except that it removes the obvious motive for her suicide. You see, we did know about Charlotte Perkins Gilman's note: mother had mentioned it to us more than once. She may have mentioned it to other people, given her views on death which Archer says you've read and agree with. So do I, of course, and so does George, my brother.''

"Veronica mentioned the note to me as though she alone held the key.''

"Well, the police didn't exactly make a point of the matter. I doubt if looking at the whole note even occurred to them. Once they found out who Charlotte Perkins Gilman was, and that she was not an unreasonable person to mention in a suicide note, they didn't go into it much further; neither, I gather, did the people at the college.''

"Then I take it you and your brother were satisfied that she had taken her life? Are you saying that the note made particular sense to you because you knew she had cancer?''

"She had had cancer three years ago: breast cancer. She didn't choose to talk about it—I think hugging secrets to oneself was a hallmark of her generation, at least its women, perhaps because all the struggles were so hard. But of course she told George and me. I advised her to go to Mass General in Boston, which was convenient in any case, and look into the possibilities of a lumpectomy. Much less mutilating than other procedures, and in many cases as safe when followed by chemotherapy, radiation, or both. Not but that most of the doctors in the country are not still suspicious of this treatment. The doctor she first consulted certainly was—but then, most doctors are men. The procedure was a success, and as far as I knew all was fine.

"It was, however,'' she continued, "perfectly within

the range of possibility that my mother had had a return of cancer and not mentioned it. When we got her note, that was what we decided, George and I. And, as you probably know, Charlotte Perkins Gilman had had breast cancer, so that the whole thing made a kind of sense.''

"Did they look for evidence of cancer at the autopsy?'' Kate asked.

"No, as far as I know they didn't. They had no reason to. All they established was that she had died of drowning in the lake, and that there were no signs of violence on her body nor drugs inside it. But, had they looked for cancer, they would not have found it.''

"She had never had the lumpectomy?''

"Oh, yes, forgive me for speaking inaccurately. She had had a cancerous tumor in her breast which had been removed. They would certainly have found that small scar. But she did not have a recurrence, and therefore could not have killed herself for that reason.''

"But how can you know if they didn't look for cancer at the autopsy?''

"There was this new part of the journal we found. We thought we had all her papers when we gave them to the library. This was the last and most current section of her journal; she had it stuck at the back of a file of business correspondence, bills, tax information, that sort of thing. No doubt that was where she kept it, away from prying eyes, though what eyes there were to pry . . .''

"Another mark of her generation.''

"I know,'' Sarah smiled. "You must think I'm very critical of so impressive a mother. Don't doubt it, I loved and admired her greatly. But she let down her hair more to me, perhaps—that's a phrase she used to use. I know of fears, and anxieties, and self-doubts she didn't discuss with many people. I saw her as very human, and full of the conflicts of her generation: you mustn't let people know shameful things, such as that your hair had all fallen out from chemotherapy. Some-

one today would just say: 'My hair fell out from chemotherapy; I'm wearing a wig.' But despite her almost
total lack of vanity in any accepted sense of that word,
my mother could not bear to have people know she was
wearing a wig, or that she had had cancer.''

"But she did tell you and George."

"Oh, she had to. She had a great sense of honor with
people. To have kept that from us would have struck
her as wholly dishonorable. To say nothing of that fact
that, as her daughter, I must know for my own safety
that I have had a mother with breast cancer. Besides,
she wanted my help: she did, after all, have a doctor in
the family."

"Didn't anyone notice," Kate asked, "that her hair
had fallen out?"

"No, that's the wonderful thing. She had straight,
grey hair, which she simply parted and cut off all
around. When she got a gray, short-haired wig, no one
noticed, except a few people who said that she had at
last got a decent haircut. She was helped by the fact that
she discovered the lump in the summer, so all this happened during vacation time. I have often noticed that
life seemed to conspire with my mother to keep her secrets. Which," Sarah added, sighing, "is what makes
it so terrible now that all this has become so problematic, that everyone is whispering about it. Do I sound
like her? I catch myself sounding like her, and even
looking like her, from time to time."

Kate leaned back in her chair. "I suppose," she said,
"you will allow me to read the new part of the journal.
But the point, if I understand you, is that it states
clearly that your mother knew she did not have cancer
as of a few days before her death, and that therefore the
reason for suicide, which you so readily accepted, has
been nullified."

"You talk like a lawyer, but more clearly."

"Thank you. I'm married to a lawyer; he talks more
clearly than one too."

"Sorry. I'm afraid that must have sounded offensive."

"Not a bit. Anyway, it makes me feel less guilty about my reluctance to see you. I have an intolerance for doctors which borders upon the prejudiced: hell, it is prejudice. You've been a pleasant surprise."

"Likewise, if I may say so. To be frank, I thought you would be, somehow, young and aggressive."

"That," Kate said, "is the nicest thing you could have said. I'm aging and shy: I like your image and shall work to cultivate it."

"You know perfectly well what I mean. Would you like to have a glass of sherry?"

"Does everyone your mother knew drink sherry? I was thinking," Kate added, at Sarah's puzzled look, "of Veronica, who also offered me sherry. If your mother liked it, that's the first unsympathetic thing I've learned about her."

"There's also scotch. I prefer it, too. It's just that there's something about sherry that makes me feel one isn't really hitting the bottle, but just being civilized. Now who sounds like my mother?"

Sarah opened a cabinet and produced two glasses and a bottle of scotch. "I hope," she said, "you don't mind it straight. I don't yet run a proper bar with ice, though I hope to one day. Right now it's all one can do to pay one's malpractice insurance. Thirty-six thousand a year, if you can believe it."

"I find I can't believe it."

"Well, no doubt it keeps us honest. I brought up that impressive figure only to keep from talking about Veronica. No doubt you're enough of a detective to have figured that out. Cheers."

"Did you know Veronica well?"

"Not very. And, oddly enough, what I knew I liked, at least in the beginning. Before she sued my mother, I mean."

"Archer never mentioned that whole episode to me until after I returned from Clare College."

"I know. We had decided to leave it out of the biography. You see, it really had little enough to do with my mother. It was Veronica's problem. And it's not that unusual. Daphne Du Maurier was sued several times."

"So Archer has been telling me."

"But then Veronica started her campaign maintaining that my mother had been murdered. That she would never have committed suicide, certainly not without telling Veronica, certainly she would not have left such a note. The last point, in the light of the new-found journal section, I have to agree with. She knew well enough about Gilman: why leave such a note?"

"Perhaps because she wanted you to think that she killed herself because of cancer, when really, it was for another reason?"

"I hadn't thought of that. It's disturbing, but less so than assuming she's been murdered, which I absolutely refuse to believe. Who would murder my mother?"

"Frankly, I've met or heard of at least six people who would gladly have murdered her, if they could have done it neatly and got away with it. Not even counting Veronica."

"You're not serious."

Kate smiled. "I've learned this in a long, hard life, partly devoted to the study of crime. Most of us think of killing: if Freud is to be believed, civilization itself depends on our sublimation of that innate desire. But every now and then, someone does. And every now and then, someone catches him. Or her. Most often, I suspect, not—so we never know. But there is this: when you find someone as loved as your mother was, by people as various as Bertie at the college, and Veronica, and Archer, and Herbert, posthumously to be sure—a person so loved is also likely to be hated."

"Yes," Sarah said. "I see. I still trust it will all turn out to be some silly mistake. But I have to face the fact that either my mother killed herself for no good, or at

91

any rate, discernible reason, or someone killed her: what a god-awful alternative.''

"Not forgetting the fact,'' Kate added, ''that if someone killed her, they must have found that wonderful thing: a drug which leaves no trace in the body, or which the pathologists didn't know to look for. That's not allowed in the best detective fiction.''

"I don't believe it happens in life either,'' Sarah said. "Would you like to come home and meet my daughter and husband?''

"It would be a privilege,'' Kate said, and meant it.

Chapter 9

I have much more experience than I have written there, more than I will, more than I can write. In silence we must wrap much of our life, because it is too fine for speech, because also we cannot explain it to others, and because somewhat we cannot yet understand.

RALPH WALDO EMERSON

*W*hen Kate reached home that evening, she settled down with the new-found, last part of Patrice's journal. Having spent the evening with Patrice's daughter and her husband, Kate approached Patrice with a new intimacy. Your daughter's is the new life, Kate wanted to say to Patrice: husband an academic and cherishing every moment he can spend with the baby, as though a miracle had offered him some unimagined experience. How would you like to climb Mt. Everest, someone might have said to him; such, at any rate, might have been his fantasy. But who would have thought the chance to nurture a baby would strike a young man as the South Seas struck Gauguin? And Sarah herself, doctor, mother, loving her husband with a kind of surprised wonder that Kate well remembered in her early married time with Reed. No one really understands marriage, Kate thought. Love either begins then, or never. And if it does not begin, tolerance and mutual desires

93

provide a fair imitation. But for Sarah, love had begun. Sarah, according to the revolting jargon of the young today, had it all. What would Patrice have made of such a phrase? Patrice would have known, Kate surmised, that no one who seems to have it all supposes herself to have it all. The sense of having it all belongs only to the future or the past, never to the present. Later, when all the things one is supposed to desire have been and gone, Patrice might have said, with one of Woolf's characters, what now? Then, perhaps, for a moment, one has it all.

As Kate had left Sarah's house, Sarah had come with her to the entrance hall, and stood for a moment, seeking the words to say something she did not yet know how to say. Kate recognized the condition. "It wasn't easy," Sarah had smiled at Kate, "to have a mother like mine. Oh, it is easy in so many ways. George and I learned as we grew up that there was much foolishness we had been spared. We were both astonished to discover, in high school and then in college, what idiocies most parents could make of their children's lives and their own. But my mother was such a powerful personality; without ever meaning to, she struck you if you were her daughter with the force of a gale wind. It was a bit easier for George, I think. He loved and admired her, but there was something between her and me, because I was a girl, because I was the first born, that gave her a power over me I hated her having. Oh, she never took advantage of it, not consciously. But she didn't understand, I think, the effect of just her presence, of her slightest word. I'm not explaining this very well. And then, when it seemed she had chosen to die rather than suffer recurring cancer, I was saddened, bereft even, but in some way few people would understand, relieved. I mean, she had chosen death, she had not lived to be humiliated by illness or age, and I knew she would not blame me for my relief. I wanted her to understand my feelings because I wanted her to forgive me for feeling them. There was more space for me when she was gone. And I was free to love her. How incomprehensible all this must be.''

''Not a bit,'' Kate had assured her, standing in her coat and wondering why it was easier to say the hard things at intermediate times, in intermediate places. ''I can't imagine what it must have been to have a mother like that, as I've told you. But I can imagine the rest, how you felt.''

''But now, you see, that we've found this last journal section, we know she didn't have cancer, didn't have that reason to kill herself. More than that, the trust that was between us, the trust I thought was in the note, was in fact not there. She didn't write what I thought she wrote. And I find I want to know what happened. Or, as the psychiatrists might say, my separation anxieties have revived.''

''It never occurred to you to find out about the cancer when she died?'' Kate had asked. ''As a doctor, I mean, or as a daughter?''

''As neither. It never entered my head. But now, you see, I must know. I'd be relieved, grateful, if you could find out. I'm glad I like you. What you do is after all not that different from what I do: we both gather all the facts we can, and then try to find an explanation to fit. Sometimes we're right, sometimes wrong. Sometimes we can do something about what we discover, sometimes not.''

Kate nodded. She had stood with her hands thrust into her coat pockets, waiting for Sarah to finish. We will have other conversations, Kate thought, but they will never have the pure intensity of this one. Patrice would have said: now you're talking.

''I can't bear, '' Sarah added, just as Kate removed her hands from her pockets, having waited out a long silence, ''for her not to have the chance to tell her part of the story. Someone has silenced her, or caused her to silence herself. I want to know why. Oh, not just for her sake; for mine, mainly. I want to be free to love her as one should love the dead, not always trying to explain to them what isn't explicable. I had hoped at first," she went on, "that the baby would be a boy, because I wanted someone to have with me the relationship George had with our mother: loving, uncomplicated, open. And then I thought, no, women have had every reason in the world for wanting sons; I shan't invent a new one. And then I came to want a daughter so much I would have felt betrayed if she'd been a boy. And yet, if I'm as good a mother as Patrice, my daughter will feel this way about me."

"She will love you," Kate said. "If she loves you as you love Patrice, well, I'd settle for that. And if I come up with some marvelous explanation, you'll be the first to know. After Archer and Herbert, of course."

"Of course," Sarah had laughed.

Kate took up the journal. And to think, we supposed we knew her; we knew all there was to know, Archer, Herbert, Sarah, me. And now there is this. We never know it all; we only make up stories about it, and sometimes our characters seem fully developed; but they have only fooled us again. And if we call ourselves biographers, we call the stories and the characters we have invented biography.

"I have just heard a story, [Patrice had written] no doubt apocryphal, but possible. Bertie told it to me. These friends of his with several children had been stuck in their country house after days of rain. And suddenly the children had found something to do, and the man slept, and the woman read. Later they found what had kept the children amused and quiet for so long; they had spent the hours in the pantry, removing the labels from every can. There, on the shelves, gleamed rows of silver-colored cans; some large, some small. No clue to what was in them. Cooking assumed a whole new aspect of surprise, and innovation. And I thought: that is how it is with people now, for me. Their wrappings are gone. I must commit myself to what is within, unlabeled. Middle aged myself, elderly really, like Strether, and George Eliot's Mrs. Transome, and Forster's Henry Wilcox, and other literary characters who are fifty-five and called elderly. If only I were artist enough to convey the incredible sense of possibility I feel, of wonder. James conveyed it in Strether, of course, but then the whole point about Strether was that he hadn't lived.

"But I shall live, it appears, for a while at any rate. The cancer has not spread, or returned, or done any of its fearful things. And as I leave the hospital, I think with a kind of wonderful joy: six more months of real living, before the next examination. But I have clearly determined, in my own mind, that it is doctors I fear, hospitals, illness, all of that, far more than death. I never go to the hospital without marveling at the people one sees who have bought life at any price. I shall never cease to wonder that life itself has a value, that death holds such terrors.

"How everything leaps out at me from the books I read. So I note that Virginia Woolf wrote: 'But I wanted—how violently—how persistently, pressingly, compulsorily I can't say—to write this book; and have a quiet composed feeling: as if I had said my say: take it or leave it: I'm quit of that: free for fresh adventures—at the age of fifty-six.' And then there is Isak Dinesen's motto, which was Pompey's address to his crew: *'Navigare necesse est vivere non necesse.'* It is necessary to sail; it is not necessary to live. She understood it, Dinesen did. My god, do only women understand it? To have done it, to be free to sail, not to worry about living, to worry about living without adventure.

"People wonder at my talk of death, I can see that. It is so hard to make people understand that if it is the future you think of, then death must be a part of that future. It is perhaps because people fear death so that they return always to the past. Or can I speak of death because I am without nostalgia? Not only do I not wish

97

to return to the past or re-create it; I have forgotten it. Would the psychologists say I have repressed it? But I think one returns to it compulsively only when one has not got control of it; when it still dominates one, when it is still the best dream, the best possibility. George Eliot wrote to her friend Barbara Bodichon, 'At present my mind works with the most freedom and the keenest sense of poetry in my remotest past, and there are many strata to be worked through before I can begin to use *artistically* any material I may gather in the present.' Yet she too, when she was an assured artist, stopped living in the past and writing in it. By the end I think that she too was absorbed in creating out of the present, out of fears for the future, possible stories. Yet surely it was rather late in her life that she wrote that sonnet sequence called 'Brother and Sister' where she longed to be a little sister again. Even the woman who created Maggie in *The Mill on the Floss* could want that. What do I want now? Only to be gloriously fifty-eight, and to write if I am so blessed.

"And, of course, I wonder about Clare, and if it will survive, and where the courage will come from we will all need. So many women are afraid, and who can blame them? And men are afraid of losing whatever manhood has bestowed. I take particular pleasure in disliking that damn classics prig: as though what the Greeks had written were somehow in danger of being betrayed by modern interpretations. It is the most durable of literatures: what do they think they have to protect it against? It is themselves they are protecting. Ancient Greek or one's own memories—in protecting them, one guards against the future."

Kate put down the journal. She had suddenly the sense of having talked with Patrice. So they had shared a good deal, since Kate's visit to Clare. And I, like her, Kate thought, have never much looked back. And I had supposed myself the only one without nostalgia, unpossessed by the tales of infancy. Odd, Kate thought. Perhaps she asked me about God, not because she hoped to believe, but because she wondered if she was alone in her terrible disbelief in the sanctity of the past. Could she have thought that only those who believe in God look to the future and even to death with hope, with wonder? She should have asked me, in that damn airport, if I was given to nostalgia.

Reed came home that evening bearing two bottles of French champagne and a jar of Russian caviar. "Celebration," he announced. "Columbia Law School next year: criminal procedure. I wonder how different it will be from my law school days at Harvard. I'll put these bottles in the freezer to get really cold, and then we shall lap up the caviar with spoons and be wholly dissipated."

"There will be more women students, for one thing," Kate said.

"Well, that's a blessing anyway. And if the glimpse I caught today of the student body is any indication, the men no longer wear three-piece suits to class. They don't even wear ties; they barely wear shirts. It must come as a dreadful shock when they go to work for Debevoise & Plimpton and have to buy a whole wardrobe at one fell swoop. Kate, is something wrong? One of the many wonderful things about both champagne and caviar is that, unopened, they keep. Are you feeling the opposite of celebrating?"

"I feel like celebrating . . . never more. Your midlife crisis had me worried, not least because it took Patrice to make you talk about it."

"And you are brooding about Patrice, that specialist in mid-life crises?"

"Not brooding exactly, Reed; wondering. How little we know of people, as I keep saying without its really having come home to me before. How did she respond to her husband's violent death? I don't know; I didn't even think to ask her daughter Sarah, whom I met today: that's another story. Then there is this law suit. I mean we all keep reading about people who claim to have had their ideas stolen; I learn from Archer that there's a whole record of cases of this sort, though I never thought about it before. There are all the powerful feelings about her at Clare: well, strong people evoke strong feelings, but would everyone go on talking about someone who drowned, however dramatically, in a college lake? I remembered Patrice with great vividness once Archer and Herbert had recalled her to me, but I hadn't thought of her again from that time to this. Do you see?''

''I can't say that I do.'' Reed said. ''And I'm not sure you do either. That's the problem, isn't it? Do you think champagne might help?''

''It can't hurt, can it? And I am pleased about you as a professor. What odd and wonderful turns life takes.''

''As we were saying about Patrice's life,'' Reed called over his shoulder, disappearing into the kitchen to retrieve the champagne.

Kate, in a manner which she devoutly trusted would have sent her sisters-in-law off into a state of slight hysterics—not that it took much—began lapping caviar off a spoon, delicately to be sure, but who eats caviar pure? ''What I was thinking of,'' she said, leaning back with her champagne, ''is Patrice's sense of being free to sail.''

''Sail?'' Reed asked. ''Can that be how she drowned?''

''Sorry,'' Kate said. ''Be patient; my brain is clearing nicely. It was a motto of Isak Dinesen's Patrice liked: 'It is necessary to sail; it is not necessary to live.' From some Roman; the original, at any rate, was in Latin.''

''When you really worry me,'' Reed said, ''is when your brain begins to clear.''

Kate grinned at him. ''Sarah mentioned that Patrice was secretive; it was a matter of her generation. Women hadn't really learned to be open with one another, I think, and they had thoughts perhaps not wholly comprehensible to males, however sympathetic and understanding. I've often thought that about Virginia Woolf. Certainly Patrice didn't seem to chatter on about what one might consider the big moments: her husband's death; that law suit; breast cancer; and—I have come, my darling to the point, sifted as I knew it would be through champagne and caviar—she was hatching a new book, whatever it might be: a new idea, the great excitement of starting something; she was ready to sail. Do you see?''

"And where, you wonder, is that book, or evidence of its beginnings, or an outline of its wonders to perform?''

"You always put things so exactly; a rare and enviable talent."

"It may have been the merest beginning of an idea, you know," Reed said. "We are all, I think, superstitious about just-conceived creatures, book or flesh, are we not? Women, perhaps, especially?''

"You are suggesting that whatever plan she had, whatever new adventure, it was still just a whisper, a breath of hope, no need to write it down, just that first, glorious excitement when everything seems possible?''

"Yes, that's what I mean, allowing for the difference in our explanatory style.''

"Shall you be very busy in the next months, before leaving the DA's Office? Finishing things off, I mean, undertaking the lugubrious task of separation?''

"All right, all right, I shall complain no more of your style of explanation. Put in words of one syllable which dogs and cats can read: you want to be absent while I, frantically busy, fail to notice or, at least, to miss you too much.''

"I thought I might spend the spring break at Clare. Nosing around, you know.''

"But haven't Archer and Herbert 'nosed around'? As her biographers, surely they have asked all the questions of all the people?''

"In a way, perhaps. But look how many new facts

they've been handed, just lately. Veronica's hanky-panky; the new journal indicating cancer was no part of her death; the emergence of anti-Patrice feeling now that the subject of gender studies has surfaced at the college, to say nothing of the new-found perils of single-sex education.''

"Where will you stay, while sleuthing around Clare during your spring break?" Reed asked with a sigh, re-filling their glasses.

"Oh," Kate said. "I'm sure the president will be albe to suggest something. There's been serious talk of the task force meeting for an entire week to finish up. I suspect the president had something to do with that week coinciding with my break. I think I shall go up to Clare and stay. Somewhere with all the amenities of civilization, and no one noticing when I come and go, or wondering where to.''

"That," Reed said, "is the chief amenity of civiliza-tion. But I," he added, "shall notice that you are gone.''

The president's secretary, to whom Kate presented her request on the telephone the next morning, seemed neither surprised nor perturbed at the question of where Kate would stay. She called back some hours later to say that the president would be pleased if Kate would be a guest in the president's house. They were quite used to putting up distinguished visitors, no one else was expected, and Kate would be most welcome. That settled, Kate arranged for a final dinner with Archer and Herbert, in order, as Kate put it, that they might synchronize their watches.

"Chinese, I think," Archer said. "Elegant food with fortune cookies at the end, I feel we need all the good omens we can collect.''

"And if they are not good?" Kate had asked.

"Be sensible, my dear. No restaurant, certainly no oriental restaurant, is in the business of ruining the digestion of its patrons. Their omens are either good, or irrelevant."

But Archer, when they were settled in the Chinese restaurant, had more than omens; he had news. "I have decided to come with you," he said. "To Clare College. You to sleuth, I to pursue biographical details. Should our paths cross, so much the better."

"I am relieved," Kate said, "just to have someone to consult each day, not to mention someone as altogether cheering and witty as you. But what about poor Herbert? Can't he come too?"

"Poor Herbert indeed. His spring break is not, like thine and mine, set firmly in March in the middle of the semester. Herbert's institution observes religious holidays, and its break must encompass Good Friday, Easter, and Passover. We shall have to give Herbert each day what the French so appropriately call a *coup de fils*."

"Particularly appropriate," Herbert said, "considering Patrice's fascination with her *coup de vieux*."

"If you are going to babble on in French, my dears, I shall have nothing further to do with you," Kate said, "And do, please, let's avoid the analogy of sleuthing, as you so quaintly put it, and biography. The answers to the mysterious questions I have begun to ask myself will loom, I think, rather minutely in a biography."

"Let us not, I implore you, argue about the metaphysics of biography," Archer said. "I think we shall not have a biography without the truth, nor perhaps the truth without her biography, though in the end, truth may turn out to be immaterial to the story of her life."

"My views exactly," Kate said. "Shall I call the president and ask her to put you up, too?" Kate asked him.

"Heaven forfend, my dear. I shall stay with Bertie and Lucy, from whom I have a standing invitation to sit at their hearth and lie in their guest room. You and I

103

shall meet for consultation on some neutral turf each day at, say, six; drinkie time."

"Can't we meet for a brisk walk around the lake?" Kate asked.

"My dear, remember to whom you are talking. Brisk walks indeed."

"What I can't understand," said Herbert irritably, "is how you stay so thin when you never stagger farther than the nearest wine bottle."

"Well," Archer said, raising a wine glass, "here's to Patrice's biography."

"And to her death," Kate said.

Chapter 10

Only those can genuinely marry who are already married. It is as though you know you are married when you come to see that you cannot divorce, that is, when you find that your lives simply will not disentangle. If your love is lucky, this knowledge will be greeted with laughter.

STANLEY CAVELL

*I*t was Kate, however, who, once she had settled in the president's house—a simple matter of being shown to her room by the president's secretary, delegated to meet her for the purpose—relaxed at the hearth with Lucy. Afterward, she would go to Ted Geddes's house for dinner. He had left a message with the secretary inviting her to spend her first evening with them, and the secretary had offered to telephone Kate's acceptance. Archer had gone off in pursuit of biographical materials associated, Kate hoped, more with life than death. It was a cold March day, and Kate appreciated the fire and Lucy's comforting presence.

"We have great faith in you," Lucy said. "Mostly because you come from the outside and will not be swayed by our murky past and complex present. Archer, too, is above it all, but Archer, apart from a constitutional disinclination to offend anyone, has to keep his lines clear for biographical purposes. You, we trust, will ferret out the truth. And please," Lucy added, "don't tell me the latest theories of narratology by which there is no such truth. You know perfectly well what I mean."

"Perfectly," Kate said. "But I need your help. Are there, I ask myself, so many dramatic events in every life? Patrice's husband was mugged to death; she was sued in court; she became a best-selling author; she was thoroughly disliked by those threatened by any assaults on their favorite ideologies. All this apart from her profession, family, friends, and daily living; in all of which, I gather, she was particularly rich. Was hers, do you think, what a friend of mine who believes in Vedantic religions calls a karmic existence?"

Lucy laughed. Although a delicate woman, she had a hearty laugh and a warm manner; she did not seem to regard herself as fragile or of limited energies, though she looked both. "Have you ever tried telling anyone your life, just a few chosen events, shall we say? It's remarkable, really, how once one consents to live, life does happen."

"Yes," Kate said, "I see what you mean. But it has recently occurred to me how little I know of her marriage. Did you know her husband? Did anyone? It was only on the plane coming up here that I realized I had never even discussed him with his daughter. Odd, that."

"It wouldn't have been true when he was alive," Lucy said. "We can only guess about marriages. I have often thought they resembled volcanic mountains, giving little warning of eruption, and revealing little of the causes after they have scattered fire and ashes."

"I like the way you talk," Kate said.

"Do you? Bertie says I have a great reputation for wisdom in certain quarters because I have rediscovered the cliché. He's right in a way. I have learned one can go far with intellectuals if one keeps a firm grip on the obvious, and announces it from time to time. But about

Patrice. Bertie did tell me that he and she rarely talked about their marriages, and I'm sure that's true. It's one of the characteristics of long friendship between a married man and a married woman. All I can give you are my observations, seasoned with a few tidy projections from my own experience. Okay?''

"Okay," Kate said, enjoying her.

"I think it was what we call a good marriage. Meaning: they trusted one another, had faith in one another's judgment and sense. But I suspect they had gone the way of most marriages like theirs: he had got out of the habit of talking to anyone, if, indeed, he was ever in it, and she had discovered women friends, in additon to male friends like Bertie, and got out of the habit of talking to him. Oh, I don't mean they kept secrets from each other. I just mean that if you've had a long and open conversation with a woman friend about the perils of male colleagues or the infirmities of women colleagues, there isn't much point in repeating it all over again at home. Much easier to talk about the dinner, or let your husband tell you the latest in his profession, which in the case of Patrice's husband, was law, and he was very interesting on the subject; I've heard him.''

"So she didn't pine when he died?''

"Of course she pined; she broke her heart and raged at the world that had killed him so needlessly. Well, I do see what you mean. Perhaps she didn't pine. Certainly she didn't, as so many women in their fifties do, seek about for another man and either find him or mark time in his absence, perhaps for the rest of life. Patrice had lived inside herself for a long time, is my guess. And once the horror had subsided, and the long grief, she knew she could make it on her own. Knew, futher-more, though one could never say so even to oneself, that here, again, was an opportunity to explore experi-ence intensely. Do you remember when Arthur Koes-tler committed suicide? Past seventy-five he was, and ill with several slowly fatal and disabling diseases. But his

107

wife in her fifties went with him. We shudder at suttee, but we seldon distinguish between bereavement and abandonment. Patrice was bereaved, but not abandoned.''

"I suspect," Kate said, "that that was how she had begun, perhaps after her husband died, to look at death. That one lived with it on honorable terms, did not fling oneself into its arms, but knew that, as with a husband, it had to dwell at the center of life. Why is it I sound ponderous, and you sound sensible?"

"Because I am talking about marriage, and you are talking about death. I'll tell you something else, though. I think when Patrice went on to have a fine life, to write her books and teach her classes and even turn into a radical on the campus, people became annoyed with her—at Clare, I mean. It wasn't proper, somehow. It wasn't becoming. To turn into a best-seller was bad enough: success always worries academics, when it moves into the popular world. But to become a revolutionary too, to question the verities, well, my dear, as Archer would say . . .''

"I take it that was President Norton's point of view, as well as that of the classics department, et al.''

"Now President Norton is something else, as our cleaning lady says. She is young, ridiculously young to be a college president; she is a lawyer. Have you ever asked yourself what that means, or how she got there? Oh, brains, of course, and ambition, it goes without saying. Did you know that she went from Clare to Chicago Law School, from there to some fancy Wall Street law firm, from there to Clare's board of trustees, and on to the presidency? Stopping along the way, of course, to marry someone equally situated, endowed, accomplished? Ask yourself what it means? She has never knocked about. She has never, as my children say, hung out. She has never taken any chances or lived an unprotected, unprivileged life. Oh, I'm not just talking about money, I'm talking about everything. As one of my friends said, she has never spent an hour in a masochistic relationship. She came along just in time to benefit from the women's movement, to have a third of her law school class women. If anyone told her that a few years before there had been only a few women in a class, it didn't register: she hadn't fought for it. She learned to get on with important, powerful people, but she never learned to listen to those with slightly unorthodox ideas, or if she listened, she didn't care, not really. Patrice could have offered that woman a rare opportunity for growth; instead, Norton treated her as though she were some sort of radical twerp, and listened instead to the honored classics professor you met here. And that is what the matter is with women's colleges, or anyway with this women's college. It's afraid of the unorthodox. And that, futhermore, is the longest speech I have ever made. You inspire me, apparently.''

"Not I," Kate said. "Patrice. There are some of you here who have come, I think, to realize what you have lost. I suppose there was never a thought of making Patrice president?"

"My dear, she wouldn't have touched it with a barge pole. They wouldn't even let her be the faculty representative on the board of trustees, where she might have been of use without giving up her life to administration. Do you know what it is? Colleges and universities are being run now by administrators, and those faculty they seduce, or persuade. Ideas have become foolish; we work on expense accounts and what will bring in the students and the donors. This means, of course, that in a women's college, you are careful not to seem to be questioning the family, the place of women, old views of God."

"What you need," Kate said, "is a drink. Does Bertie agree with all this?"

"He says he does. No, that's unfair; he does. He's stood up with Patrice against a lot of foolishness. But he, too—certainly since Patrice died—has started flowing with the tide, treading water, whatever—another of my clichés. I don't think he's forgiven Patrice for deserting him."

"And he believes she did. Desert him, I mean. Kill herself."

"I think," Lucy said, "the way things are going, he's beginning to think she did the right thing. Oh, that's an exaggeration, of course, but he's pretty depressed about life on this campus, about the whole thing. Now if Patrice were here," Lucy added, getting up to refill their glasses, "she would not have let us reach this state of gloom. She had a way of inspiriting people, giving them courage. I think there's all this talk about her death because no one can really believe she would have let us all down so."

"Do you think she would have?"

"I think she might have. In a moment when the energy level was low, and the gloom heavy. I used to comfort her sometimes, as she did me, although we talked seldom enough. There was a time when I was jealous of her, of course, but it passed."

"As she grew older?"

"Yes," Lucy said. "As she grew older, and I learned to love in unconventional ways. She really understood, Patrice did, how to turn middle age into the greatest time of life. Into adventure. I began to dream of when the children left home for good, and my hair was gray, and my shoes flat. She made you see you didn't have to buy into the dream of youth. She said to me once—I have always remembered it, because it struck me at first as down right bizarre—she said that she could hardly remember the time when her children were little; she had just barely kept on top of things in those days. But now, she told me, she treasured her grown children; they were friends to whom you didn't have to explain the past. And sometimes, she said, after the children had left home, she and her husband would sit together reading in the evenings, exchanging thoughts, and she felt they had leapt from loving when they were young to this moment in middle age; and that everything in between had been a play someone else had acted in, someone else had written. Oh god, Kate, I do miss her, every day. And so does Bertie. And that it wasn't disease, or accident, or crime, but her own choice, her own despair. I understand, but I shall never forgive her. Never.''

Kate walked to Ted Geddes's house by the lake. She resisted the habit, universal outside of cities, of driving everywhere. Of course, she could have skirted the campus in a car, arriving at Geddes's house from the road side. Instead, feeling eccentric as she declined Lucy's offer to drive her, she walked from the village onto the campus, and across the campus to the lake, then around the lake, almost half way, to the Geddes dock. She stood for a while on the small dock, surveying the lake and pondering, as was inevitable, Patrice's midnight swim into its middle. There were other parts of Patrice's journal to read and study; many people to see. But Kate felt that turning point, inevitable in any narrative from Greek drama to a cocktail party, when one knows how it must come out, even if one does not yet have all the facts. At what point did Oedipus know who the man was at the crossroads whom he had killed? At the moment when Jocasta hung herself, or just before? Kate recognized that most turning points are evident only afterward, when the fact that had to have been there is revealed. Psychoanalysis, she gathered, worked the same way. So Freud "knew" at a certain point, that his patients had witnessed the primal scene. Or, as a literary theorist Kate greatly admired had written: "In the case of *Oedipus,* as in many other narratives, of which the detective story is only the most banal example, the discourse focuses on the bringing to light of a crucial event, identified as a reality which determines significance." Who killed Laius? What is the memory behind the screen memory? Why should Patrice, who had been prepared to welcome death, have gone too early to meet it?

Kate walked up the rather long path from the lake, past the still-covered swimming pool, and around the house to the front where she might enter as a proper guest. But Geddes had seen her and called her in the backway, onto the porch which looked across the lawn to the lake.

"My god, you walked," he said. "For one amazing moment I thought it was Patrice; she always came that way, and stopped on the dock to look back across the lake. It is a beautiful sight, isn't it? You are rather like her, you know, not in looks, but in the way you stride along and stand with your hands in your jacket pockets. Come in, come in. I hope," he added, as he led Kate into the living room, "you aren't offended. You, of course, are beautiful and elegantly dressed; Patrice was neither. One never knows what will offend women."

"I'm not offended," Kate said. "Quite the contrary. I saw Patrice only once, but she seemed beautiful to me. May I wash?"

"Forgive me. There is a small loo under the stairs here, or a bigger one upstairs."

"Under the stairs will do very well," Kate said. And she smiled as she closed the door on the small bathroom, obviously tucked in as an afterthought. There was a time when one wanted not to be within hearing of anyone while using the facilities. T. S. Eliot would not even shave in front of his wife; but then she, of course, was mad, whether because of him or in spite of him was altogether unclear. Kate tended to think because. She recombed her hair which had been blown by winds from the lake, redoing the French knot. What *shall* we find to talk about?, she wondered, sticking in the pins. But she always wondered that, and rarely was she graveled for lack of matter. I am the reliable chatterer, she thought, turning off the light.

Geddes's wife had joined him in the living room. Kate, once introduced, sat down and refused sherry. "Would you by any chance like Laphroaig?" Geddes asked. "Patrice introduced me to it. Would you like to try it?; it's really quite remarkable."

"I have tried it," Kate said, "and would love some. No ice; just a little water. Were you very close to Patrice, then?"

"I like to think so," Ted said. "We were both, as I told you at the cocktail party, interested in life cycles and argued constantly. It was one of those continuing conversations that never ends between old acquaintances—you know, the sort you always return to no matter what you talk about in between?"

"Did you agree about life cycles?" Kate asked.

"Oh, more or less. Perhaps like everybody else, I thought youth was the best part; but we agreed on the main things."

"Well," Gladys Geddes said, sipping her sherry (she did not, she had explained, drink the hard stuff), "I thought Ted was far too tolerant of all that anti-youth stuff. Of course to be young is very heaven—didn't someone say that?"

Since Gladys had paused, apparently for an answer, Kate said, "Yes, but *when* you were young seemed to have something to do with it, and then it was remembered heaven, our old friend nostalgia. When Byron actually fought in a revolution, he was thirty-four, which he considered the very brink of desiccation, and his hair was going gray. He didn't live to be a really old man to talk about it, unlike Wordsworth."

Gladys looked puzzled. "I don't actually follow you," she said. "What have Wordsworth and Byron to do with it? It's just better to be young than old; I'd have said that was obvious."

Kate tried very hard not to blame men for their wives, but she rarely succeeded. ("Nonsense," Reed would say. "Some women are determined to be idiots despite all; and some men too, of course. Why blame the spouse?" "Because," Kate would answer, "men have an outworn model for women, and these wives adopt it and become it. Their husbands shouldn't have

113

had it in the first place." "And that, dear Kate," Reed would answer, "is such nonsense I refuse to pay it the compliment of rational refutation." "Whenever you become pompous," Kate had answered, "it's because you know I'm right.") I miss you, Kate thought. Reed, why aren't you here with me with these idiots?

"You're being a bit dogmatic, Gladys," Ted said. "Take someone like Colette. Certainly her youth was not the best part of her life."

"Then why did she keep writing about it?" Gladys asked, "and about her mother with that damned flowering cactus. I read her book about being fifty or something and turning down her lover, but in real life she snapped him up fast enough and married him. Well, didn't she? You certainly agreed with me at the time."

"I take it that Gladys and Patrice did not always agree," Kate remarked, she hoped lightly.

"Gladys just likes to argue with academic women," Ted said. "She feels faculty wives are underestimated and underappreciated. Is dinner almost ready?" he asked Gladys, obviously wanting to break up this little scene.

"In a minute." Gladys said. "The other day Ted had one of those women professors here, for lunch it was; I made gumbo soup and muffins baked from scratch, and salad. She and Ted sat around talking about gender studies or some such rot, and when she left she said to Ted; 'Well, I do think we ought to examine all sides of the question before making up our minds, and you've really helped me to do that.' And then, if you can believe it, she said goodbye to me and thanked me for the lunch."

"Really," Kate said. "How uncouth of her."

"Well, it did seem a bit pointed," Ted said.

"Have I had too much of this lovely malt whiskey?" Kate asked. "Well, thank you, just a spot more. Ought she not to have thanked you for the lunch after you went to so much trouble?" She accepted a refill with

114

the only pure emotion she had experienced since arriving. "Is it rude to thank someone for lunch?"

"As though she and Ted had had a businessman's lunch and I was the cook, or hostess, or something. Don't you see?"

"Didn't you want Ted to ask her to lunch?" Kate asked. I'm missing a clue here, she said to herself. Something wrong here, somewhere.

"Of course," Gladys said. "I help Ted with his books. He's ready to admit that, aren't you dear?"

"But of course he is," Kate, who thought no such thing, hastened to say. This, clearly, was one of those marriages. "We all know professors whose wives do all the research, and typing, and sometimes even write the book. I could name ten such without even dredging. Are you saying the woman professor snubbed you at lunch?"

"No. But why thank Ted for the conversation and me for the lunch? Don't you see?"

"No," said Kate, who had meant to say yes. "I mean, you made the lunch, so she thanked you for it. If Ted had made the lunch, presumably she would have thanked him." I can't, she thought to herself, believe I am having this conversation, if you can call it a conversation. "Well," Kate tittered, "I shall be careful not to thank you for the dinner."

"Which I will get," Gladys said, sweeping from the room. "Don't drink yourself blind with that dreadful stuff," she said. Clearly, exit lines were her specialty. And what line can possibly top that? Kate asked herself. I absolutely insist on drinking myself blind in your dreadful presence?

"Is March too early to fill the swimming pool?" Kate idiotically asked. If the pause got much longer it might become the eternal silence. "How *do* you fill it? With a hose, or do you take off the cover and collect rain water?"

Ted laughed rather nervously. "With a hose. And not for several months yet. Since," he added rather fiercely, "it doesn't rain enough all year to fill a swimming pool, rain would not be a practical method."

"About as impractical," Kate said, "as looking forward to being old. Do you miss your youth?"

"Yes, I do. I prefer the energy of impetuosity to the mellowness of wisdom."

"And Gladys agrees."

"And that, Professor Fansler, was not a nice remark."

But you enjoyed it, you son-of-a-bitch, Kate thought. You don't like her any more than I do. Frankly, I think she ought to take up mellowing the way some people take up needlepoint. "Sorry," Kate said. "I was merely referring to her stated preference for youth. But since I agree with Patrice on the glories of middle age and of Laphroaig, do you think I might have a speck more? As I was telling my husband just the other day, we drink too much. Did Patrice also? Drink like me, I mean, not mention it to her husband, who was dead of course, or mention it to mine whom she never met." Kate held out her glass and, silently, Ted Geddes filled it.

"Tell me more about your work," she said. "What exactly are your findings on the life cycle?"

Ted told her. When, summoned by Gladys, they went in to dinner (freshly baked biscuits, Kate noticed: I must remember not to say thank you), he continued to tell her. Occasionally Gladys added a bit. Ted had been at this study for a long time—he was unusual as a social scientist in having been funded for a longitudinal study that would enable him to follow his subjects for many years. It would emerge soon and make a big impact, Kate somehow gathered. Not to have gathered it, as she reported later to Archer, one would have had to be, not blind drunk, as Gladys clearly thought she was, but unconscious.

Indeed, so riled up and depressed all at the same time was Kate when she left the Geddes's—Ted had insisted on driving her to the president's house—that she had waved him goodbye from the porch, and walked over to Bertie and Lucy's to find Archer. And so impressed was Archer with her condition that he actually agreed to take a walk with her. "But not around the lake," he said. "In this dark, we will only fall in."

"I'm sure now Patrice walked in on purpose," Kate gloomily announced. "If I didn't know I could leave here at the end of a stated period of time, guaranteed to be less than ten days, I'd walk into the lake myself. My god, what a place."

"It must have been a delicious dinner," Archer said, "if the food matched the conversation."

"It always does, haven't you noticed?" Kate said. "The only thing they couldn't spoil was the Laphroaig, and they had a good try. Creamed chicken on rice, actually."

"Ah," Archer said, "the sort of food that is fattening without being comforting. Well, I had an excellent dinner, all because of the good conversation with Bertie and Lucy, if you insist, and what's more I've had a mysterious phone call. About which I am sworn to secrecy in the best possible manner."

"Tell."

"Tomorrow. After I've talked to him. I promise."

"No fair hiring a detective and keeping secrets from her. Do you know, Archer, my love, I'm to have dinner with Veronica tomorrow night, and I'm positively looking forward to it . She may be prickly, but she's not petty or stupid. I do think people should either be nurturing or informative."

"No," Archer said, "like food, they should either be comforting or delicious. And occasionally, even both."

Chapter 11

*Verisimilitude is the collective, anonymous voice whose
origin is a general human knowledge.*

ROLAND BARTHES

*T*he next morning the task force again got underway. This time, however, those, including Kate,
who were willing at least to consider the question of
gender studies had done their homework. They presented ideas and arguments, and the discussion bore
some relation, Kate thought with relief, to a scholarly
undertaking. By late afternoon, the entire group, having talked their way through a working lunch and a surprise presentation by the director of women's studies
from a neighboring college, was at least willing to consider the possibility that a women's college ought perhaps to offer, in its curriculum, some organized
questioning of gender ideologies. Whether this should
be accomplished by urging all professors to introduce
such questions in their classes, or by special classes ded-
icated to these matters had become, by five o'clock, the
central question, heatedly debated. Kate considered
that this was progress. At the same time, her attention
had, as the afternoon wore on, drifted toward Archer

and his mysterious informant. Kate half expected to be called from the room with a message, and when the meeting broke up she scarcely knew where to go to await Archer.

But as she descended the path from the administration building, she met Archer hurrying up it.

"Ah," he said, "I'm so glad we met. I didn't know whether I would have to haul you out of your meeting or pace the floor waiting for you, like an expectant father of yore."

"Why of yore?"

"Well, I, of course, am innocent in these matters, but I rather thought that fathers nowadays assisted at the births, or were anyway present, if they didn't deliver the babies all by themselves. And a very good thing too, I'm sure."

"I see what you mean. Where shall we go to hear your news. The nearest bar?" she asked hopefully.

"Do you know, Kate, my dear, I think we had better trot around the lake. At a seemly pace, of course. We must not be overheard, and somehow to retire to your room at the president's house with a bottle, firmly shutting the door behind us, hardly strikes the right note, do you think? If I can walk, can you do without a drink?"

"I'm not as bad as that," Kate said, shoving her hands in her jacket pockets and striding forth. "I am without thirst and all ears."

"Well, don't let's gallop, I implore you, or I shall have no breath left. The man who came to see me was a doctor. Patrice's doctor, in fact. He was as nervous as peas on a hot shovel—"

"As they used to say of yore."

"Yes. He had heard at a dinner party that I was writing Patrice's biography and was, furthermore, staying at the college while investigating her death. Not too jumbled, I suppose, for dinner party news. Anyway, after an agonized day and a sleepless night, he decided to talk to me. Better me than the police, he said, and if I turned out to be unreliable, he would simply deny having said a word. He was close to frantic, really, and not the frantic sort basically, or so it seemed to me.''

"Go on," Kate said. "You mustn't stop so often to breathe.''

"Well, the question is, I suppose, whether to believe him at all. But unless he's absolutely bananas, which seems very unlikely under the circumstances—oh, lord, I'm out of breath and what's more, as I tell this to you, it does sound as though I might be a victim of a practical joke.''

"Let's sit," Kate said.

"A lovely idea, but on what?''

"The ground, you urbanite. Lower your bottom to the ground and lean against a tree.''

"Wouldn't it do something irreparable to my trousers?''

"Archer, pull yourself together. What did the man say, for the love of heaven.''

"You must let me start at the beginning and go at my own pace, snaillike though it may be.''

"Fine. Only Veronica is expecting me at seven, so if you haven't got a bit more into the swing by then, I shall have to telephone." Archer looked around as though he expected to see a phone booth on the next tree.

"It's getting rather dark, isn't it?''

"I know what I shall do," Kate said. "I shall call for Herbert. Clearly, you can't be trusted out without him.''

"I'll be all right." Archer sank to the ground. "It's like this. This doctor met Patrice at someone's house, and they got to talking. Somehow, she found out he was a doctor, maybe he told her, at any rate, she called him the next day and asked might she come for a conversation—''

"A consultation?''

"That's what I asked. No, she said a conversation, but she added that she would expect to pay him as though it had been an examination or whatever. He made an appointment for some days after, and she came. He lives, I should add, in a suburb of Boston and has his office in a building near his house, but not attached to it. A renovated barn, I think he said; we'll have to go to see it if I don't turn out to be hallucinating, or if he doesn't. Anyway, the point of all that comes later.''

''Married?''

''No, since you ask. How clever of you—I didn't think of it for hours. If you want to know, I suspect he's gay, but he didn't say so, and nobody seems to take any notice of it. Shares his house with a musician. Does all this matter?''

''Only to the extent that it seemed likely he wouldn't be your run-of-the-mill beastly doctor if he attracted Patrice. But I was inquiring less about his sex life than about his conventionality. Go on.''

''Patrice duly called him and made an appointment at which she asked him, were he to become her doctor, what were his minimum terms.''

''By which, I take it, she was not referring to Medicaid.''

''He was bright enough to understand that immediately. In fact, he's really quite bright, for a doctor, if I can assume we share the same prejudice against the medical profession. She wanted to enroll herself as his patient, but without having to be examined from head to toe, to say nothing of the more horrible inbetween. She simply wanted someone she liked and trusted to call in case of an emergency, the possible recurrence of her cancer, or a need for pills of some sort. Well, it turned out, he had heard of her; he'd even read *The Years of the Red Cat* and loved it. And she told him about Auden, who couldn't have a doctor who wasn't a friend, and who had to do without one when his doctor friend died.''

''So he agreed to her 'minimum terms'?''

''More or less. He understood that she hadn't been

121

happy about the way her breast cancer had been treated, at least at first. Her original doctor there had been one of those pompous I-know-everything-and-you-know-nothing types, the kind who evokes the question, whose body is it anyway? This chap did request permission to take her blood pressure, test her blood and urine, and listen to her heart and lungs, all without her undoing so much as a button. He found everything fine except her blood pressure, which was high, but Patrice said it always was when she visited doctors, not to worry. You know, the ground is remarkably ungiving. I bet those outdoor types never pause without inserting an air mattress between themselves and the hard, hard earth.''

"Have you not read *Antic Hay* by Aldous Huxley? Well, would you rather walk after all? One moves the legs and saves the bottom.''

"What I would rather do is take a bottle up to your room and close the door and let the president think what she likes. I can't imagine what induced such an uncharacteristic frenzy of discretion in me back there. It's this bloody place, of course.''

"We've got to walk half way around the lake to get to the president's house, so keep talking as we go.''

"Whatever you say. Oh my city streets, where are you? Well, all the tests turned out okay, and Patrice had a doctor, and, in fact, recognizing a friend when he saw one, he asked her to dinner once, and that was the only other time they met. Now, my dear, comes the sinister part.''

Archer paused to brush a leaf from the top of his shoe where it had heedlessly settled. "We are now, dear Kate, at the summer before last, the summer, that is, almost a year before the June in which Patrice died in the lake. She was spending the summer here in her house, working on . . . well, it isn't too clear what she was working on. You might take that up, in a casual way, with Veronica. But she simply stayed home, or strolled sometimes to the library.''

122

"It was probably the book she quoted Virginia Woolf about," Kate said. "In her last journal. 'But I wanted—how violently . . . [and lots of other adverbs] to write this book.' *That* must have been it."

"No doubt. Whatever *it* is. All went well, that summer, but after a time she began to get what she thought was a summer cold. She had a sore throat that wouldn't go away, and she seemed low on energy; you know, fluish, only without the fever or the end-of-the-world feeling. She finally mentioned this to someone who urged her to, for god's sake, see her doctor. And so, having decided to trust her doctor, she went to see him. At least, she telephoned. His recording machine answered, and she left a message that she would be over during his office hours the next day."

"And she went?"

"She went."

"And what did your nameless doctor find was wrong with her?"

"I don't know, and neither does he. Because he didn't see her. He was in England at the time."

"Archer! A plot. At last we have something that tells us something."

"Ah, my dear, but does it? It's one of those stories, I'm afraid, that peter out sorrowfully without ever coming to anything as dignified as an anagnorisis, let alone a peripeteia."

"I shall push you into the lake in another moment, I promise. This, however, is the president's dock, from which she might paddle a canoe if she had the time or the energy, so you are saved. Let us creep up, sinfully, to my room. Though why we should act so furtive I can't well imagine. A more innocent biographer with his personal detective could scarcely be dreamed of."

It was, however, greatly to their relief that they met no one on the stairs or in the hallways. Archer expired with a great sigh into an easy chair, and Kate produced a bottle of the by-now-inevitable Laphroaig from inside a locked suitcase, extracting the key, as dramatically as possible, from her pocket. "The loveliest thing about this divine stuff is not even its taste, but the fact that it can be drunk, with no diminution, straight from one's toothbrush glass. We take alternate sips. Go on, for heaven's sake," she said, handing him the glass. "Even if there isn't a dénouement, something must have happened, or why would the doctor have risked all to tell you?"

"Thirty minutes till you must leave for Veronica," he said. "What nectar that is; I shall become addicted, at least while resident in women's colleges. Well . . . when Patrice arrived the next day at the office, there was another doctor there, behind the desk. He said he had got the message, that he was taking over for Dr. Myers (all right, that's the name, but I have sworn on my mother's grave to tell no one, so you must be discretion itself . . .)."

"But Herbert told me that your mother is almost as charming as you are, present tense."

"Let us not quibble. We must be careful, dear Kate. The man is really trusting us."

"Archer, you ought never to become jittery, it is not your style. This other doctor was taking over from Dr. Myers . . ." Kate added in a whisper, to encourage him.

"Well, Patrice didn't really want to talk to him, but he suggested that she take a good deal of vitamin C, et-cetera, and request some antibiotics from the infirmary at the college should she have a fever. Meanwhile, he just wanted to take some blood to be certain it wasn't something or other . . . you know the style. And Dr. Myers would be back in a couple of weeks."

Archer held out the glass for a refill, and offered Kate the next sip. "He had, however, this substitute doctor, taken her telephone number, and he called to ask her to come in again to see him; something in the blood. So she drove over, and he told her that he thought she ought to know that, according to the preliminary tests, she had cancer of the pancreas. He said he wanted to check again, and perhaps they should consult someone he could recommend at Mass General, but he was afraid the diagnosis was indisputable. He would not have told her, but cancer of the pancreas is an extremely virulent cancer, and often leads to rapid death. He managed to suggest the death was also painful, etcetera. This is how Patrice told it to Dr. Myers, and how he told it to me.''

"What did Patrice do?"

"She went away to think about it. She had to decide whether to call her daughter, or to go to Mass General, where they had treated her before, or what. Meanwhile, a week went by. Finally, she decided to call this substitute doctor to ask for something, and Dr. Myers himself answered the phone. His musician friend had learned in England that one of his compositions was to be performed, and he came back to work on the orchestration or something, and anyway, Myers had come back with him. And said, 'Get the hell over here this minute.' To Patrice, of course.''

"And?"

"Surely you can guess. He had left no one as a substitute, he never did. His practice was covered by another doctor in the area when he was away. No blood had been sent to the lab from his office while he was gone. Furthermore, he told Patrice, no one would decide one had such a frightful cancer, or any cancer, on that evidence, nor, he felt certain, could the imposter have been a doctor. Of course, Myers examined her, did tests, etcetera. Her sore throat was better by then anyway, but it is not uncommon for cancer of the pancreas to first show up in that way.''

"I know," Kate said. "I've known several cases at the university."

"She didn't have any sort of cancer, of course. And Dr. Myers was really on the spot. Just think, Kate. Someone had broken into his office, advised one of his patients, left no sign, and taken nothing. And, apart from Patrice's story, there wasn't the smallest evidence

125

that any part of this had even happened. What was the man to do? He liked and admired Patrice: but the whole tale was so unlikely. Myers was certain no doctor could have been induced to take part in any such farce, and, anyway, what would have been the point? So it had to be one of two things; either there was an absolute imposter who had trained himself to draw blood well enough to fool a patient who'd had a good bit of blood taken in her time, not to mention all the rest of the rigmarole, and what possible motive could he have had? *Or* Patrice was just a little bit balmy. Well, of course once the idea had entered his head, he allowed himself to hear any available gossip about her, and as you well know . . ."

"So he decided Patrice had made the whole thing up. Damn him, anyway."

"Kate, darling, ask yourself. Besides, he didn't exactly decide, he just kept an open mind."

"Always easier to believe in a gaga older women, than in a man's perfidy. I've seen it many times."

"Said she darkly. Well, of course you are right, as Myers now suspects."

"But I bet," Kate said, "that when she killed herself, or appeared to have killed herself, he concluded that he had been right about her all along and put the whole matter from his mind. No doubt she told him her theories about not allowing yourself to wander helplessly into old age, and welcoming death, à la Stevie Smith, and all that. And however unusual he is, no one can speak so openly of death without bringing their sanity into question. As you well know. I bet what he felt at her death, more than sorrow, was infinite relief."

"No odds. But then, you know, and you must try to give him a little credit, he heard all these rumors about her death, and he did begin to remember how much he had liked her, how she had struck him as whole, and genuine, and unlikely to go in for any such nonsensical folderol. But by now it was almost two years later, and what an idiot he would sound if he told this story to anyone official. I think he's been quite brave to come to me, and I think you should talk with him—after I've persuaded him to trust you—and erase that frown from your lovely forehead.''

''I shall be late for Veronica. Perhaps I can get her, in the most casual possible way, to shed some light on this dangerous game.''

''Be careful Kate.''

''I'll try. But it was child's play for anyone to break into his office, particularly in the afternoon. If neighbors had seen someone there, he would just have said he had orders to come in and paint or clean the carpet or something. Whoever he was, he wasn't taking many chances. But who was he? Someone we know, do you suppose?''

''I consider it highly unlikely. In fact, impossible. For one thing, Patrice didn't recognize him.''

''True. And we are unlikely to have met anyone she wouldn't have recognized. Too bad, I was beginning to have hopes for Professor Fiorelli, or the husband of the antifeminist classicist.''

''That's not impossible; the husband I mean. I ask you, my dear, seen once, forever forgotten—the most unmemorable person.''

''Archer, you have raised my spirits immeasurably. Don't you see what we know now? We know that someone wanted Patrice dead, and took what seemed a clever way, damn clever. Let her think she had a nasty, painful, and incurable kind of cancer, and—well, knowing Patrice—couldn't he count on nature, meaning Patrice's nature, taking its course? That failed, and he tried something else.''

''What? Can he have impersonated yet another doctor? No to mention the inevitable question, why did he want her dead? I mean, if I plotted to remove from this earth everyone at my university who particularly offended me—you take my point.''

''I do. But suppose a chap who particularly offended

you had suggested that he would gladly blow his brains out if, let us madly narrativize . . .''

"Kate, never did I think I would live to hear you use such a word. 'Narrativize,' indeed.''

"Let us say your imaginary colleague had often announced that if he found his wife had been unfaithful he would blow out his brains. Wouldn't you be a teeny bit tempted to make him believe she had been unfaithful?''

"You go to Veronica, my dear. I am going to try to set up an appointment for us with Dr. Myers. And try not to narrativize, I implore you. Shall you reconnoiter before we slip guiltily from the room?''

"Don't be silly,'' Kate said, opening the door. She shut it immediately. "Hold on, the president's on her way up. Do be quiet,'' she added sternly, as Archer began to giggle. "Well, I admit it is funny, in a way, but I expect I shall appreciate the humor better when we are safely in New York telling this story to Reed and Herbert. Oh, lord, I shall be really late for Veronica.''

Kate, after all, having run all the way, was not really late. Veronica greeted her in a calm and cheerful manner, which Kate was grateful for and puzzled by. Had she ceased grieving or had Kate's presence on the campus somehow comforted her? The latter, it soon transpired. Veronica had faith in Kate, and believed she would discover who was responsible for Patrice's death. Veronica and Sarah, Kate thought; pray I do not fail you both.

They sat down at once to dinner, Kate having declined a cocktail and declared that she was starving. She determined to go straight to the point. "Forgive me,'' she said, "if I seem a bit relentless in my questions, but if you don't believe that Patrice wrote that note, and if you don't believe she would have taken her own life, even during a time of sudden despair, who do you think killed her and why?''

"What sort of time of sudden despair?'' Veronica asked.

"Well, suppose she'd just heard she had a fatal and painful disease. Suppose she had learned she was going blind, or had decided the book about which she was so excited was worthless; you make up the plot. All I ask is: aren't there some circumstances in which Patrice might have sought death? As Woolf did, for example?"

"Some, perhaps. But remember Woolf's notes, to her husband, and to her sister."

"Patrice left one to her children. I do not mean, forgive me, to suggest that you were unimportant to her, but as Woolf demonstrates, one tends to leave notes to one's family."

"I don't really want to argue the point," Veronica said. "Let's just say the whole thing didn't smell right to me. The question is, what can we do about it? What can you do about it?"

"I can think about your ideas for suspects, just for starters. Remember, you are accusing someone of murder."

"I'm prepared to do so. Well, if you want my opinion, and I'll trust you to decide what it's worth, I think it was a woman. Definitely."

"Why? The smell of it? The way detectives in novels fifty years ago used always to say: 'Poison is a woman's crime,' etcetera?"

"Well, I don't stereotype crimes, but yes, the smell of it. For one thing, a man could have overpowered her; a woman couldn't. Patrice was in her fifties, but she was in good shape, a vigorous woman. Also, she tended to trust women, even beastly ones. Of course, she set it up for them with her talk of death. Remember, it happened in June, at reunion time, when the place was overrun with women. Including the president, and I don't discount her as a suspect, not at all. I think Patrice was a real pain in the ass to her. I know, I know —how did she manage it? But that's not what you asked me. And then there's another reason I think it was a woman. Men still feel themselves in power, certainly around here. There are many ways the system offers

129

them to get rid of disturbing women; they don't need to kill. Oh, they might kill in anger, but they wouldn't plot to kill. Easier to plot to undermine and defeat, in all the ways our institutions offer."

"Veronica," Kate asked, changing the subject, "can you offer me one reason for women's colleges these days? I mean, we all know how important they were in previous times. But what proof is there now that women do better in an all-women college?"

"Oh, just the sciences are reason enough. Women go into science in far larger numbers from all-women colleges. I don't know why—you want me to guess about everything tonight. But it certainly has to do with the male ambience in coed schools somehow preventing women from trying to be scientists. It's all a matter of cool statistics. Just look at where your women scientists went to school. Math anxiety is a problem enough for adolescent girls, without adding leering, jeering males to the problem in college. That's what it comes down to, I guess. In a women's college you don't seem to be asking women scientists to question their womanliness. Patrice understood all about that, by the way. Oh lord, what Patrice understood."

"Well, apparently her devotion to women's education at women's colleges was enough to keep her here. She'd been teaching for the whole year, hadn't she, before her death?"

"Oh, yes. Reunions always coincide with graduation. Those more recent classes having reunions would want to look up Patrice, if they had studied with her when they were here. It was a hectic time, following the end of semester. She was a bit tired, I think, but no more than usual."

"The summer before she had been ill, hadn't she? Feeling fluish, with a sore throat?"

"I wasn't here during the worst of it, but that's true. Fortunately, she had found a doctor she was willing to consult, which made me worry about her less than I had."

"Do you know what she was working on that summer?"

"Not exactly. She didn't like to talk about her work, but one always knew when she had a project underway that had captured her. You could almost see her filing away sudden thoughts or observations for use."

"I think not talking about one's work is quite usual. Tucked up in my cozy room in the president's house, I've been reading the marvelous letters of Sylvia Townsend Warner—too many snippets when I like whole letters, but what marvelous snippets! She writes to tell someone about her biography of T. H. White, which she began when she was seventy, and asks for the project to be kept secret, explaining: 'I hate having my doings known. I have a superstition that it brings ill fortune on them.' That's probably how Patrice felt."

"I'm sure it is. But it was exciting her, whatever it was. About women's lives, I feel fairly certain, just judging from her conversational gambits."

"That gets a lot of attention in the journal too."

"I envy you having seen it. Oh, I know, I could have gone and read it in the library where it's housed, so long as I didn't take notes until after the biography. But somehow, I knew I couldn't bear it. And, to be frank, I suspected also that she never wrote about me, and that I might feel hideously offended, stupid as that sounds."

"Not stupid. But I can assure you, there are few persons mentioned in her journal, at least the recent sections that I have read. She seemed mostly to be grappling with the idea of the present as the absolutely important moment."

"Perhaps," Veronica said, "that is what she was writing about. How is the task force going, speaking of the present?"

"Better. At first we just heard a lot of growls and snarls about the very idea of gender studies. But lately, we're acting quite grown up and looking into the matter, like sensible folk. A great relief, I assure you."

"If you're responsible for the change, you should be officially commended by the college. It's one of those dreary histories. A group of feminists on campus, young faculty and students—what the alumnae call 'radical feminists' with a knowing look—sent a petition around to all the departments, asking them to introduce at least one course concerned with women. What a storm; you never heard the like. The faculty, mostly male but ardently supported by established females here and there, wrote to the alumnae, the trustees, wailing that lesbians were trying to take over the college; really my dear, as Archer would say, they quite ran out of nouns and fell back on hideous adjectives. The result is no one's said boo about gender studies, until the president decided to have a task force. Someone had written in a journal that Clare was the only college of renown, single sex or not, with *no* women's or gender studies program. If anyone has now managed to consider this with seriousness, you are a remarkable woman."

"Not I, I assure you. It's just that, when an idea's time has come, not even those whose reactions are the most impassioned can stem the tide forever. Thank you for a lovely and most welcome dinner."

"Next time you must bring Archer. I'll promise French champagne when you find Patrice's murderer."

"I'm glad to hear you say 'when,' " Kate, departing, called back. But even if we find this doctor impersonator, *if* he exists, she said to herself darkly, how much closer are we? And if we can't find him, or know if he exists, how can we find the murderer or know if he or she exists either? Why couldn't Patrice have been one of those who said with Montaigne, "Let death find me planting cabbages"?

Chapter 12

We are in the power of no calamity, while death is our own.
THOMAS BROWNE

*T*he next day Kate, dragging her guilty conscience behind her like a leg manacle, cut the afternoon session of the task force to meet Archer and Dr. Myers. Reminding herself that her main reason for being enticed to the campus was the investigation of Patrice's death, she nonetheless hated to leave the task force just as it seemed to have decided to replace prejudice with exploration. This morning's discussion had eventuated in an invitation going out to at least six women directing women's studies programs or women's research institutes, and the afternoon was to be devoted to planning these forthcoming confrontations. Kate excused herself on the grounds of a prior academic commitment, and hoped she would not be found at the wrong moment disporting herself with Archer in some inevitably unsuitable place.

Archer was at his most ebullient. "Dr. Myers awaits us," he said to Kate, handing her into a car he had borrowed for the occasion. "If we decide that he is a disappointment in any of several possible ways, I suggest we just murmur that Patrice's death can only be accounted for stochastically, and exit on an airy note.''

"I'm not going to ask what it means, so you might as well tell me straight off,'' Kate said, as they drove toward Dr. Myers.

"It is a *much* nicer sounding word than narrativize and means pure chance, wholly at random. I understand that it is used by statisticians, and that a computer can be trained to it: picking, say, a series of numbers wholly at random: stochastically.''

"Nonsense,'' Kate said.

"Have it your way. Either someone narrativized Patrice into the lake, or she was compelled thence stochastically. You know, a lot of random little events caring less than nothing for each other, conspired, or rather didn't conspire, to drown her.''

"I'm beginning to wonder if you've made this Dr. Myers up out of whole cloth, done it just to annoy, like the boy who sneezes. He does exist, Archer, doesn't he?''

"If not,'' Archer remarked with considerable satisfaction, "we have made a wonderful fiction of him.''

But he existed, in a building separate from his house and reached by its own driveway debouching into its own parking area. He had been waiting for them and came to the door as they were getting out of the car.

The first thing that became eminently clear to Kate, and greatly simplified the whole discussion to follow, was that she understood immediately why Patrice had liked him, why he had appeared to her as the sort of doctor that does not come in bushel lots. He seemed devoid, to start with, of a professional manner, being a person of great warmth to those he liked and, Kate could guess, a certain sangfroid to those he didn't. And those he liked, Kate was prepared to guess, combined high intelligence and a distinct originality of manner. A despiser of pigeon holes and typecasting, he was, one would have thought, the last person to be replaced at his own desk in so cavalier a fashion.

Dr. Myers led them into his office and, Kate noticed, unlike the president, sat behind his desk after placing them in chairs set before it. As though we were patients, Kate thought; he wants us to understand the ambience.

"I have racked my brains," he said, "quite literally. Tortured them, stretched them beyond endurance. I started with three possibilities: Patrice lied, or imagined the whole thing; I, in a frenzy of fabulation, imagined she had told me this; someone impersonated a doctor in my office, leaving no trace. Apart from my faith in Patrice and in my own sanity, there seemed little to help choose between them. This thought was so unbearable that I set out to establish the impersonator: I searched, that is, for a trace of his presence. And, my friends, I found it."

Kate became aware that she and Archer had received this news with identical expressions characteristic of those who have just won a lottery. Good, Kate thought. I want to believe in him; and I want him to have believed in Patrice. Odd, really, how important to us all is our faith in her. More than anything, we fear discovering that she has betrayed our love.

"I started," Myers said, "as you will no doubt be amused to hear, as Freeman Wills Crofts. Fingerprints, tire marks, ash dropped from esoteric cigarettes, witnesses who saw him here. None of the above. I'm sure there are fingerprints here that may be his, but who is to say whose they are, except that they are not mine? The same with tire marks. As to anyone's being observed, the old lady in English novels of the more refined sort who sits at her window and sees everything had nowhere to sit, though I don't doubt she has her being in many English streets. It is, in fact, so deserted around here during the day that burglars' vans have been known to drive off with the entire contents of someone's house, unnoticed and undeterred. I turned my attention to the office. Unfortunately, the extremely efficient woman who manages my office for me had done a thorough job of cleaning and sorting while I was gone, and I think that our impersonator must have come after she had finished. One of the idiot facts is that I don't know exactly when Patrice saw him; I was so *bouleversé* about the fact of her seeing him, that *when* she saw him didn't seem, at the time, to loom as a very large question. And then I had my first bit of luck. I asked Marjorie when she had cleaned the office, and she said, just before I returned, it was dumb luck that I didn't come back before she'd even begun. Her father, it turned out, had broken his hip and she'd gone to stay with him a bit. That meant, of course, that she'd done her thorough turn-out *after* the imposter. I brightened considerably at that, because Marjorie is the sort who would notice if the cat grew an extra whisker.''

He paused as though waiting for a comment, but Archer and Kate merely willed him on. ''Well, of course, I took Marjorie into my confidence, where in any case she resides, and implored her: 'Did you find anything, anything at all out of line, even the slightest, smallest detail that seemed, however minutely, to jar?' Nothing came to mind, but she asked me what I was looking for. We know, I said, that he came dressed to impersonate a doctor; he brought his own device for taking a blood sample: mine were untouched. He must have driven here in his own car and left in it. He connected and disconnected my recording device. He may have changed his clothes before he left. Marjorie went off to commune with herself, and then called me several hours later. *She* turned out to be the great detective.''

''The recording device,'' Kate said.

''Ah, but I gave it away to you in my telling. I, of course, didn't think of it at the time.''

''And neither did Archer nor I think of it,'' Kate said. ''He had to have fiddled with it.''

''Exactly. I had rather hoped for some blood on the rug, or the glue he had used to stick on his false mus-

136

tache in the bathroom basin, but it was the recorder that did it. It did, at least, definitely establish his presence. Or someone's. Because what the tape in my machine said when I left was: 'Dr. Myers is away for a month. Dr. Quelque Chose at this number is covering his practice. Please call Dr. Quelque Chose for any matter requiring immediate attention.' For the impostor to be sure that Patrice did not get that message, he had to substitute another tape. One which said I'm out of the office, please call back or leave your number. He would have had no trouble finding that tape in my desk drawer. Needless to say, he erased all messages from my regular tape before departing. But: here's Marjorie's thought. While he had the wrong tape on, the one that lured Patrice here for my putative office hours the next day, someone else may have called and got it. Someone else may, at least, have got a message saying I would call back; and, of course, I didn't.''

"And so the blessed Marjorie called around?"

"Exactly. With some cock-and-bull story about the recorder having malfunctioned and needing evidence to get them to fix it, or something. She found two people, two, who had called and got, not the vacation message with the substitute doctor's name and number, but the one saying I would call back when they left their number. Needless to say, I didn't. But when they called again, they got the vacation tape and figured, well, the old boy really needed the time off.''

"Hallelujah," Archer said. "Glory to the most high.''

"It's not as glorious as all that," Kate said. "All we know for sure is that Patrice wasn't doing a put-on for whatever reason, and I knew that already.''

"Ah," Archer said, "but the beauty of proof for those of little faith.''

"It also means," Dr. Myers said, "that we can go after him. We have evidence instead of the word of a dead woman, and our unsubstantiated confidence in her.''

"Be honest, Kate," Archer said. "Or perhaps," he added, turning to Dr. Myers, "I should ask you to be honest. Without that evidence, mightn't there always be the nasty suspicion that Patrice *might* have made up the story for reasons of her own?"

"I am being honest," Kate said, "also relieved. As far as I'm concerned, it chiefly means that we shan't have to go searching for an actor with experience as a paramedical. That's a relief, anyway."

"Why not?" Dr. Myers asked. "I certainly would like to find him."

"We know the important thing: that someone tried to kill Patrice, or induce her to kill herself. To me that means only one thing: that he tried again, and succeeded."

"How and why?" Archer asked.

"Don't trouble me with details," Kate grandly answered. "At least we know she didn't walk into that lake of her own free will. That's what matters."

"Let me say something as a scientist." Dr. Myers swung around in his chair, allowing him to stretch his long legs out in front of him. "From your point of view, it doesn't matter who hired the imposter, I can see that, not if you can catch her killer by other means. But, quite aside from the affront to me of having my office used so cavalierly, I think you ought to try to find who was behind this little game. Should it ever come to trial, evidence of a previous attempt at hanky-panky would certainly sound well from the witness box."

"I take it," Archer said, "we can be absolutely sure it was the same person."

"Little is absolutely sure, even in science," Dr. Myers said. "But if we have to contemplate two lunatics hating Patrice enough to conspire her death so indirectly, we had perhaps better reconsider if we know all we ought of her."

"There is always the possibility," Archer sadly suggested, "that someone conspired once, in impersonating a doctor here, and that the second time she really

138

did decide on suicide, perhaps depressed to discover anyone hated her so much, or fearing ever to hear that she did have some awful cancer.''

"What are you trying to be," Kate asked, "the idiot child? In fact, you are begining to sound like Herbert. Are you suggesting that in some frenzy of sainthood, she decided to rid the earth of her polluted self?''

"Who is Herbert?" Dr. Meyers asked.

"Herbert," Archer answered, "is my collaborator who is about to turn detective, or, at least, to hire one. I agree with you, Dr. Myers. We ought at least to attempt to find out where this fake doctor came from. You seem to assume he was an actor, or was that Kate's assumption.''

"It must be right, in any case," Dr. Myers said. "It takes a certain amount of training to carry off that sort of impersonation.''

"Why don't you look for someone in 'General Hospital'?" Kate said.

"Clever remarks will get you nowhere." Archer smiled. "I think we ought to hire someone, a private eye if you'll excuse the expression, to go around to the actors' agencies and make inquiries.''

"Have you any idea what that will cost?" Kate asked. "I agree with you, he probably came from New York, but what a job. Excuse me, but have you a doctor-looking actor on your books who knows something about medicine from his real life, and could be hired for a private enterprise, slightly illegal but well paid?''

"Why don't we try anyway," Dr. Myers suggested. "Let me pay for it, at least at first. It matters to me personally, in the first place, and I may be able to sue the hell out of whoever did this in the second place. Then, when you uncover whatever plot there was to do in Patrice, my information will help your case. But I wouldn't mind if Herbert hired the private detective; better on the spot, I should think, than by long distance.''

"I'll talk to him when we get back," Archer said. "But you do realize that the culprit may well be someone from around here with acting talent and a connection to Patrice undreamed of by us. Are you sure you want to risk the money, Dr. Myers?"

"Let's start with the likeliest odds, anyway. And do call me Dirk, won't you? Can I offer you a drink?"

"Is it possible," Kate asked, "to hypnotize someone and tell them that when they wake up they will walk into the middle of the lake? No, I thought not. Did you say a drink? Might I also have a cigarette, without hearing about the medical dangers of either ill-advised pursuit?"

Driving back to the campus sometime later, Kate announced to a somewhat distracted Archer that she wanted to get straight exactly what was going on at Clare College on the day and night that were the last of Patrice's life. "It was June," she said, "and that's about all I know."

"And there were reunions, classmates, cavorting about and recognizing one another behind the wrinkles and fat."

"I can always tell when you're worried," Kate said. "You descend to cynicism."

"Well, Kate, I ask you. Here we have a perfectly marvelous woman, a good friend and a good writer as someone said once of a spider, or so I am told by my literary friends with progeny, and everything handsome about her. True, she courted death, but not in an outrageous way. As Stevie Smith said, 'I often try to pull myself together, not knowing whether other people find death as merry as I do.' I can't go along with Herbert's definition of her as a saint, but she was full of courage, and intelligence, and genuine kindness. If we thought she had a reason for killing herself, we eliminated it, or rather them: it was neither age nor incurable illness. I'm talking myself into a muddle."

"Did I tell you," Kate asked, "that I'm reading the

letters of Sylvia Townsend Warner? I'd only just got to page one-fifty, when I discovered that she actually found drinkers congenial. Now there's a woman I would like to have known well, second only to Patrice, of course. She said of drinkers, 'There is a generosity in their recklessness. We had a drinking old lady as a neighbor for many years, and I had the greatest esteem for her because she knew what she wanted (not many women do).' I think the important thing about Patrice was that she knew what she wanted. Why was that so threatening to someone?''

"Kate," Archer said, driving up to the entrance of the president's house to let her off, "I'm feeling muddled and unhappy. I thought getting this all settled with Dirk Myers would make me feel better, but it's made me feel worse. It's as though I were losing Patrice, and finding myself in the middle of a novel by Simenon. At any moment a man in a derby will round the corner and tell me he was at school with me, and his jewels have been stolen. I want to get back to the biography: I want Patrice back.''

"We'll be back in New York soon, and you and Herbert will get to work again. You haven't lost Patrice, my dear, you've just undergone the shock of discovering the academic world in its perhaps anachronistic form as a women's college. I'm dining with Madeline Huntley tonight, and before that I'm going to request from the president, or anyway her minions, *all* the facts about that June day Patrice died. I don't, of course, think it will do a bit of good, but I shall, at any rate, have finished the task force by tomorrow and shot my bolt. Dear Herbert, dearest Reed, here we come. You go back for now to Lucy and Bertie and let them cheer you up with their domestic bliss.''

"I'm not in the mood for domestic bliss. Would you like to go into Boston and visit some night spots?''

"Archer, be good. It's just a question of what Sylvia Townsend Warner calls the fatal law of gravity: when you are down, everything falls on you.''

"Do me a favor, Kate, will you? If you refuse to cavort with me in a properly frivolous manner, at least read another book."

Kate, going up the president's steps, grinned at him.

Chapter 13

A saying of Leonard's comes into my head in this season of complete inanity and boredom: "Things have gone wrong somehow." . . . We were walking along that silent blue street with the scaffolding. I saw all the violence and unreason crossing in the air: ourselves small; a tumult outside: something terrifying: unreason. Shall I make a book out of this? It would be a way of bringing order and speed again into my world.

VIRGINIA WOOLF

*O*ther detectives, Kate said, peering around Madeline Huntley's office with a certain look of dismay, *"do* things. I've just read a book in which the criminals had the detective caught in a rock crevice—they were on the desert, of course—and they made a fire underneath, and he just managed to get out, I forget how. There was action. All I do is sit around and talk in rooms, some gloomier than others."

"That's all one does in college in any case, isn't it?" Madeline asked. "Forgive me for not being properly sympathetic; I get rather tired by the end of the day. All psychiatrists do is sit around and talk, too. That's all anyone does, except workmen, and most of them stand around and talk, is my experience."

"Clare is getting you down," Kate said. "It seems to get everyone down."

"Except the alums, who love the dear place and grumble only at the changes. The sort of alums, that is, who go in for dear places. The others are too busy getting on with the job. Is Clare worse than most, do you think? I remember suggesting it was when we met that first day you came up here, but I'm not sure such beastliness can be unique to this college. It must be a kind of epidemic thing.''

"Have you met Veronica?''

"Of course. Veronica is one of those people one meets.''

"What do you think of her?''

"I didn't like her at first. Aggressive; someone you expect to elbow her way to the front of a bus line, that sort of thing. But she's rather grown on me, or, unlike everyone else here, she hasn't grown more tiresome. I'm afraid you've got me at the end of an even worse day than usual. I was composing my letter of resignation when you came in. Let the male Freudian convinced of penis envy take over: he'll have his work cut out for him. I don't think there's a student here *clever* enough to envy a penis, and that's the truth. What were you asking me about?''

"Veronica.''

"Let's get out of here, Kate, and go to Boston, and eat an extremely expensive dinner. I promise to concentrate on your questions the whole time.''

"If you want to drive over an hour for dinner, who am I to quarrel with you? How shall I get back?''

"I'll put you up for the night and drive you back in the morning when I come to work. You can help me compose my letter of departure. Oh, don't worry, I've everything you could possibly need, except a solution to your mystery. Ready?''

"Hadn't I better leave a message for the president in case she notices I'm gone?''

"She won't notice. And if she does, maybe she'll have the lake dragged. That woman has as much imagination as a vole.''

"What's a vole?''

"It's a mole without imagination. The car's in the

parking lot, a mere mile away. Douse the lights, will you?"

When they were seated elegantly at a table over which hovered the wine waiter, summoned by the maitre d', Kate insisted upon Madeline's giving her attention to Patrice's death. "I've humored you," Kate said, "to the point of coming off without so much as a toothbrush. But you have to help me. We were talking about Veronica, if you remember. You're a psychiatrist. Do you think she would kill the thing she loved? You know, I take it, about the suit against Patrice."

"I do. She came and told me about it recently. There are several odd points. First of all, that Patrice more or less forgave her. I mean, I agree that Patrice was just this side of the angels, but one would have thought she would maintain a certain distance from someone who had sued her into next week, and on such grounds. Apparently, after a while, Patrice resumed a sort of friendship with Veronica; I think it can all be explained by Patrice's having determined not to make policy, but to deal with each thing as it came. She might not consult Veronica so freely again about a book—I don't think she did—but why deny yourself a friendship which, let's face it, must have been a mite more stimulating than most of what passes for human relationships on this campus. The other odd point is that Veronica really believed, I think, that she had played an important part in the conception of that book, even in its writing, and she wanted Patrice to acknowledge the fact. You would not believe, my dear, how we long for parents, or their substitutes, to acknowledge our importance. My father, who will never see eighty again, thinks that I am serving the devil doing psychiatry and am a political radical into the bargain. I know in my calmer moments the old coot is a reactionary fool, but I still dream of his saying, 'Well done, my child.' "

"But how did Patrice become Veronica's mother? Anyway, Veronica loved her mother, she told me that, so presumably Mama had said, 'Well done.' "

"Presume no such thing. Rack of lamb, I think. The sort of solid food one hasn't eaten since the children left home, and, anyway, everyone's a vegetarian these days, especially at Clare. It's their idea of a cause, and enough to turn one into a cannibal. Where was I? Mothers. You see dear, the psychiatrist, me, is used to the phenomenon of becoming the good mother so that the real mama can be the bad mother. Patrice must have become the good mother for Veronica, but don't quote me. Why are we discussing mothers?"

"Why are we discussing anything? Madeline, why is it that listening to the head of women's studies from Brown or Princeton talking to our task force can make me absolutely gung ho about women, convinced of the fact that changing gender ideology is the most profound revolution around, and yet when any of us has spent more than a day at Clare we are ready to fight for the exposure of all female babies at birth? Is this some deep problem with my psyche, or is there something profoundly wrong with Clare, and perhaps all women's colleges?"

"There is absolutely nothing as soul satisfying as pâté on toast points. Is it really delicious or just fattening and reassuring?"

"I had exactly this conversation with Archer, and I insist that you stop talking about food. Eat, drink, but talk about Clare."

"Kate, I already told you what I think, didn't I, in that smelly tunnel all that while ago? Read Margaret Rossiter on women scientists in this country. Just as science became a hard discipline, women became conceived of as everything the opposite of hard: soft, loving, wifely, charmingly irrational. So there was always that conflict. Rossiter points out that when Emma Willard started her school she had to pretend to be turning out better wives, better domestic companions and mothers, while teaching some real subjects. Did she know what she was doing? Was this double message conscious? Rossiter doesn't know and neither does anyone else. But women in education have always been caught in this bind. Their feet have had to be bound, symbolically speaking, whatever the culture. And the woman who liked hard facts had to be thought, and had to think herself, unwomanly. Nothing's changed. Try to teach gender studies and the male faculty will assure the alumnae that the college is being taken over by lesbians.''

"What do psychiatrists make of this great fear of lesbians?"

"If they're Freudians, they make of it what he did; they're scared out of their jock straps or girdles, as the case may be. Read all the latest interpretations of the Dora case, that is, if you have a spare month. What I don't understand is why all those women who see life as either happily orbiting around a man or miserably floating in outer space without one don't welcome lesbianism: it takes that many eligible women out of the zodiac, if you follow me."

"If women's colleges aren't concerned with women's advocacy, what are they doing, except protecting the male idea of womanhood?"

"There, you see, Kate, you put it better than I do, and in a third the words. Can we go on to something more enlightening, such as another bottle of wine? Do you mind switching to red to go with my lamb?"

As the waiter changed the glasses and removed the pâté plates, Kate leaned back and sighed. Why was this conversation with Madeline so much less fraught, less tense, than any conversation, even with Archer, on that damned campus? She kept returning to that same question which was not, after all, her business. Her business was to find out what had happened to Patrice that June night. Ought she to ask Madeline about the

Dr. Myers impersonation? Not without getting Dirk Myers's permission, and Kate was fairly certain he would want the story to go no further, at least for now.

"Kate," Madeline said, "I am now feeling better, and shall turn my attention to your problem. You've been very patient with my bad temper. Your problem, if I may state it boldly, is why did Patrice walk into that lake, and if she didn't walk in, how did she get there. Right?"

"Right. Madeline, you were in medical school before you became a shrink. I man, you *are* a doctor. Is there any drug that would render someone unconscious but not be found in the body hours later?"

"Of course. Sodium pentothal. It dissolves and disappears."

"That drug they always used to give people in movies and make them count backward? Then they would remember and tell all?"

"The very same. Called truth serum by the incognoscenti. It is, by the way, not just used to evoke a hidden memory. It relaxes, etcetera."

"What you are telling me is that someone could have injected Patrice with sodium pentothal, and there would have been no trace at the autopsy?"

"Not so fast. Injections leave a mark. Sodium pentothal has to be injected into a vein. Unless you could put it in the same hole used for intravenous feedings, if the patient were in the hospital, for example . . ."

"Mightn't such a small hole be overlooked in an autopsy?"

"Not if the medical examiner was on the ball. And most of them are—I bet Reed will tell you that."

"What about in the scalp, for instance, under the hair?"

"Kate, are you planning a murder or detecting one? The scalp is *not* a good place to find a vein for injection purposes."

"Still, I'm encouraged. It proves she could have been overpowered and then left in the lake to drown."

"Except she couldn't have," Madeline said with her mouth full. "Heavenly lamb. How is the salmon papier? Papier delicately enough papiered? Good. She wouldn't have drowned in the same way. I assume that they found her lungs full of lake water. That meant she drowned in the lake; someone put into the water unconscious drowns differently, at least for medical purposes. But don't take my word for it. Maybe you're right."

"No," Kate said. "They'd have thought of that. Signs that someone has been thrown into a lake after they're dead or unconscious must be the first thing they look for in an autopsy. For a moment there, though, I thought we had it."

"Kate. Why not face the fact that she probably committed suicide? From a psychiatrist's point of view, it makes sense. There used to be an old saw about those who threaten suicide never doing it, but that's nonsense. It's quite the reverse. Look at Plath, and Woolf, and Sexton—they'd all tried it before. Plath even wrote a poem about it, didn't she? Maybe she didn't wholly intend to succeed, and maybe Patrice didn't. It was a busy night, lots of people around, maybe lots of old alums wandering around the lake, thinking of their first revolting kiss, I wouldn't doubt it for a minute. It must have been depressing as hell. And why didn't someone hear her? Hadn't she been in the water some time, which would suggest she'd gone in before the wee hours of the morning, or is that only a guess?"

"You mean that because she thought about death, courted death, wrote about death, it is easier to believe she killed herself? Granted. But let's face the fact that our knowledge of her views on death, and they were hardly undisseminated, made her murder that much safer: everyone would say what you just said. And then, Madeline, there are other reasons, which I'm not free to tell you, that suggest murder, or at least, nefarious plans."

"Be mysterious, if you want, but don't brood, at

least not here when I am about to persuade you to have crème brûllée, properly done. Let's just say, you'll consult me if I can help? Is that all right?"

"Of course," Kate smiled at her. "Are you really about to compose your letter of resignation?"

"It's half done. Not one day after June fifteenth do I stay."

"What's June fifteenth?"

"Graduation. And for some reason it's always the hottest day of the year, if it isn't pouring, or so I'm told. My contract will run to July first, of course, but I won't do much more than dilly-dally and give away my office plants for the rest of June. How long are you staying around these parts?"

"Just till the day after tomorrow. Unless I decide to stay for the weekend, which I shall only do if anything capable of investigation occurs to me. I doubt it will."

"Task force finished?"

"It will be by Thursday. And I think there is a distinct possibility that they may recommend a trial program in gender studies, for a limited period, of course. Then the president will either become hysterical with dismay or kill it outright. I'm taking bets, either way."

By Thursday, it was clear that Kate was right only up to a point. The task force did indeed recommend, not a trial period exactly, but that a program in gender studies be formed and offered to certain departments for experimental programs and classes. They also suggested, with a good deal of urging from Kate and the by-now-emboldened members not averse to the whole idea, that some support in the form of subventions and reductions of course loads be offered to those who wished to develop a course in gender studies or to undertake appropriate research. That'll do you one in the eye, Kate thought, looking at the classics professor who was in no position to apply for either. But no doubt, Kate said to herself, she'll do a total switch, and apply for money to prove there *were* no women in ancient

150

Greece. What a nasty person I am becoming; no wonder Patrice brooded on death. She couldn't, like me, just get up and go.

Kate was, however, wrong about the president, who gave every sign of welcoming the task force recommendation and invited them all to a cocktail party on Thursday evening to celebrate the conclusion of their endeavors. Kate, changing into a dress more suitable to the occasion, wondered if the president would wait until they were all gone and then either kill it or let its implementation, if that was the beastly word, become endlessly delayed. Ah, Kate thought, but I shall keep an eye on her, and write her little reminding notes. I shall warn of that tonight while refusing her inevitable sherry.

But here again Kate had been too precipitous. All beverages, spiritous and other, had been made available (not Laphroaig, of course. Odd, really, that Geddes should have picked that up from Patrice: perhaps she told him about our airport meeting, but not, I feel certain, about our conversation). Kate, reverting to the ever faithful martini, chatted to members of the task force with whom she now had that sort of bonding familiar to small groups who have undergone some dangerous and extended experience together: surviving a plane crash in the desert, for example. Kate, thinking of Patrice, decided to mention her. "Too bad, isn't it," she said, "that Patrice Umphelby couldn't be here. She would have been pleased with our results, don't you think?"

"I've often thought of that," a woman faculty member, who turned out to be in mathematics, said. "And sometimes it rather seemed to me that you were standing in for her very well. I've never really seen the point of studying gender in so deliberate a way, but I must say that all those women who are working on this impressed me very much. I miss Patrice a good deal," she added.

"Were you at her memorial service in New York?"

Kate asked. "It was certainly a testimony of someone who mattered."

"No, though I would have liked to have gone. We had a service here, of course, in the chapel. They tried to make it the sort of event Patrice might have liked, but there was too much grief, from her friends and family, and too much hypocrisy from the others. I myself," she added, polishing off her whiskey, "thought it would have been the better part of valor for them not to come."

Kate smiled, realizing how much she liked this stocky woman, who had devoted herself to theorums and not the sex life or gender of her students. It was, after all, a blasted litmus test, this liking of Patrice. Those who had liked her were the good ones, obviously. Come on, Kate, she said to herself, how many of the faculty have you met?

The president made her way over to Kate in the course of her peregrinations around the room, and they stood for a moment, each uncharacteristically speechless. Kate could scarcely mention her investigations here. The president, remembering their initial conversation, hardly wanted to launch into a discussion of the task force. "I hope," she finally said to Kate, finding her tongue first, "you have been enjoying our beautiful campus. March is not the gentlest of months here, but there are some fine days for walking."

"I particularly like walking around the lake," Kate said. "How long has the college owned all the land surrounding it?"

"Since before my time, but not much before, I think," the president said, welcoming the neutral subject graciously. "There used to be great worries that the land would be taken over by thoroughly unsuitable people, with an eye out for developments, or a swimming club, or worse, whatever worse would be. Fortunately, a wealthy alum's husband gave us enough money to buy the rest of the land around the lake. The faculty have been encouraged to live in the houses

152

there, and even to build others, though the mortage costs are largly borne by the college, and the houses revert to the college when the faculty die or leave them.''

''There must be quite a bit of competition for them.''

''There is; but, as you might expect, the older faculty who have been here longer largely own them.''

''I've visited Professor Geddes.''

''Oh yes, he's been a fine warder of his. He and his wife never stop improving the property; we actually reminded him that it will revert to the college. They put in a swimming pool some years ago, and recently they planted lawn down to the lake. You wouldn't have been able to notice the lovely effect of it in March. I do hope you will visit us later, when we will be looking our best.'' Her eye began to precede her to the next conversation in her rounds. Kate bowed her temporary farewell with more liking than she had yet felt, though whether this was due to gin or the social graces of the president was scarcely worth determining.

''I do admire the way she circles around the room,'' one of the men from the task force said to Kate. ''I also admire, if I may be allowed to say so, your skills at the committee table.''

''Nonsense,'' Kate said. ''I was merely an interloper who talked too much. But I have wondered,'' she went on, turning the conversation from herself as always with strangers, ''why do those faculty who live around the lake build swimming pools; why not swim in the lake?''

''Oh, I'm one of those who live around the lake and has a swimming pool, so I can easily answer: one can't swim in the lake. It's undergone all sorts of hideous transformation from boats, chemicals, and other things, and, in any case, it's forbidden. Accidents are far too likely, and the only way the students can be kept from swimming in it is if no one does; we do however, skate on it in the winter, and my daughter sails on it in the summer.'' Kate was grateful to see that discussion of the lake did not remind him of Patrice; an economist, he was one of those downright men who discuss the problems at hand and don't wander off into frivolous associations. Her conversation with him seemed to exhaust her tolerance for cocktail parties, as well as her social obligation to this one, so she took a casual farewell, and went over to Lucy and Bertie's, hoping to find Archer.

Chapter 14

When my mother died I inherited a house I didn't like, yet
esteemed enough to have a certain piety about selling it to
someone who would make hay of it—the more so, since her
ashes were buried in the garden. Then I discovered that two
middle-aged school teachers, who had caravanned in its
paddock for holidays, longed for it as for something
unobtainable and a fairy-story. So I sold it to them, so cheap
that my lawyer coexecutor could not speak for fury: and have
been happy ever after, flying home on my broomstick.

SLYVIA TOWNSEND WARNER

*A*rcher, Lucy, and Bertie were draped around
the fire, welcoming Clare's spring vacation, which
would begin, of course, just as Kate's and Archer's
ended. Kate told them of the glorious ending of the task
force and urged Bertie to see that the president did
what she was enjoined to do.

"Any other requests?" Bertie asked. "Like getting
the whole English department to retire, making way for
the young and inventive? How's your investigation
coming, by the way? Archer said we must wait for you
before discussing it."

"There's nothing to discuss, really," Archer said,
with less than his usual ebullience. From this Kate
gathered that the Myers matter had not been mentioned to his hosts.

"Well, I have a question," she said. "At the cocktail
party to celebrate the conclusion of our deliberations, I
was discussing the lake and the faculty houses on it, for
lack of anything else to talk about, and it occurred to

155

me that I didn't really know where Patrice had lived. Not on the lake, was it?"

"She never lived on the lake," Bertie said, "though she might have been entitled to one of the houses in recent years. But by then her children had gone, her husband was dead, and she sold the house they had all lived in and moved into a faculty apartment. Less responsibility altogether. If she wanted to go away, she locked the door and went, telling a neighbor. It was a nice, roomy apartment, but nothing special about it."

"What happened to it when she died?"

"Her son and daughter came and cleared it out—the son mainly, since the daughter is a doctor and couldn't spare that much time. They each took some of the stuff, gave a lot away, and stored what they were uncertain of."

"Then how? . . ." Kate asked.

"Sarah moved recently," Archer said. "When the baby was expected. And she took her mother's stuff out of storage, including her files. That's when she found the other part of the journal."

"Was she social with the rest of the faculty?; did she dine with them, see them much?" Kate asked.

"As I mentioned the first day we met," Bertie said, "in the course of inviting you to a cocktail party, Patrice hated those. And she didn't much like cooking. She did dine out in restaurants with people from time to time: neutral turf, she called it. I don't think she wanted to be bothered with cooking. But she and I, for example, when we weren't circumventing the lake, used to sit in her living room or mine, hers more often because there weren't children, and talk about everything. Is this all in aid of some theory of yours?"

"I only wish I had a theory, or even a bright idea," Kate said. "It's only by talking a lot of nonsense to everyone that one learns anything at all, I'm afraid, especially since one has no idea what one wants to learn. Unlike Oedipus, who at least was interested in what happened at the crossroads. I realized this afternoon that I had no idea where Patrice had lived."

"I can take you to see the apartment if you like," Bertie said. "There's someone else in it, of course. Do you think there might be a suicide note hidden under the floorboards?"

"If Patrice had written a suicide note, she would have pinned it to the door, like Luther," Lucy said. "Anyway, she wouldn't have hidden it."

"She did leave a suicide note, my dears, may I remind you," Archer said.

"I don't believe in that note, not anymore," Bertie said. "Veronica is right, I think. Archer's told us all about that," he said to Kate.

"Well," Kate said, "I don't want to see the apartment. I think I'll take a walk around the lake."

"Want any company?" Bertie asked.

"Speak for yourself," Archer said. "The next time I walk farther than the nearest taxi, it will be on cement sidewalks."

"Lucy?" Bertie asked.

"There's still dinner, for which I hope Kate will stay. Why don't you two go, and Archer and I will carouse in the kitchen."

"I think Kate would rather go alone," Bertie said. "May I join the carouse?"

Kate smiled at them, and promised to be back in an hour.

Once again, she set out to cross the campus. She and Archer would probably leave the campus tomorrow morning, and she wanted a last walk around the lovely lake. Since it had claimed Patrice's life, she ought not to have loved it, but bodies of water are oddly innocent of the lives offered to them. Kate had once explored the water meadow Virginia Woolf used to walk across with her dog, making up her books, and Kate had climbed over a small rise to the river where Woolf had drowned herself. It was not a river, really, but an estuary, salt—Kate had tasted it—with a current strong enough to carry two passing swans along. Kate had not felt then that the river had claimed Woolf, nor had the lake claimed Patrice.

This time around, Kate paid more attention to the faculty houses bordering the lake. They were widely spaced, and most had small docks onto the lake, apparently for the launching of boats since swimming was forbidden. Perhaps, she thought, some of them did swim, at night, or when the campus was empty in the summer. Could someone have induced Patrice to swim? But the campus was not empty then, quite the contrary; it was swarming with reunioning alumnae and the families of graduating seniors. Still, might someone have had an illicit swimming party? Would Patrice have been likely to join it? Kate rather thought not; it was not a middle-aged thing to do—not, at any rate, a late middle-aged thing to do.

She had reached the path by the Geddes house, where one was not allowed to thank the hostess for lunch. Kate grinned to herself, walking rather faster so as not to be noticed should the Geddes couple be looking out. What had Patrice made of Gladys Geddes? Really, Kate seemed only to be thinking of new questions, and answering none of the old ones. Under a tree, she stopped to notice the lawn the president had mentioned. Yes, one could see, it was smooth, and ran straight down to the lake path. This made the Geddes house look rather manicured, not an effect Kate cared for.

She returned to find the others had taken seriously their plan to carouse. Coming from the air and a vigorous walk, she viewed them for a moment as someone abstemious must always view imbibers. Kate found she did not like the vantage point, nor the state of mind it induced. Her presidential martini had quite deserted her, and she accepted another as she joined the hilarity in the kitchen.

158

"All the same," Archer said, drawing her into the living room as their hosts completed the dinner preparations, "I'm feeling very low, an I'll-go-into-the-garden-and-eat-worms kind of feeling. I talked to Herbert and he flatly refused to so much as look an actor's agency up in the phone book. He said no actor would undertake such a part, and if he did, it would be for a lot of money and as a private arrangement. One wouldn't just call up an agent and say, send me an actor for a little spot of criminal behavior, and make it one who knows how to take blood. I do rather see his point, don't you? Besides, where would an actor have learned how to take blood? In training for "M.A.S.H."? Where are you going?"

"Upstairs to make a phone call," Kate said. "I just thought of something. Say I'll be right down, will you? If anything comes of it, I'll tell you right away, Archer. Don't mind me, I'm restless."

Kate found a phone in the bedroom, and sitting down on the bed, dialed Dr. Myers's number, charging it to her credit card. Honesty apart, she didn't want a record of the call on Bertie's bill. Dirk Myers had given them his home number, and she found him just as he was about to sit down to dinner. "I'll only keep you a minute, I promise," she said. "If it takes longer, I'll call you back. Just think for a moment before answering. Did Patrice say anything to you definitely to indicate that the imposter doctor was a man?"

There was a long silence on the other end of the line. Kate pictured him going over in his mind the entire conversation. "I just assumed it," he said. "I honestly can't remember that she said it was a man. But I think if she'd used a female pronoun, I'd have noticed it."

"She has a doctor daughter, and would not in any case be the sort to particularly mention that the doctor was a woman," Kate reminded him.

"Let me think. I've been so certain in my mind it was a man that it's hard to remember. Of course, she didn't talk about him—or her—much at all. When she got me on the phone she said: 'The doctor who replaced you told me I have cancer of the pancreas. I've been thinking . . .' Something like that. I interrupted her and told her to get right over to see me. It was clear from her voice she was upset, not unnaturally. I didn't ask her about the doctor until later and then—wait a minute, she did say: 'I don't want to talk about it, Dirk; it was a horrible experience, no matter how you look at it.' Since I couldn't be absolutely sure she hadn't imagined the whole thing, not then anyway, I didn't want to talk about it too much. What made you think of it? I'm coming," he shouted to someone in another room.

"Just something Archer said. I'll tell you about it later. One other quick question. When blood was taken from Patrice, it must have left a hole in the skin. Could that hole have been used for an injection months, even years later, to hide it I mean?"

"My god, you are being the detective. But that plot won't do. The puncture mark would have disappeared long since. Anyway, if there'd been such a mark the medical examiner would have noted it; I gather he didn't."

"You're right; I've just fallen in love with sodium pentothal. I'll talk to you soon."

After dinner, when the cleaning-up was finished, Kate and Archer went up to Archer's room for a confab. Kate told him about her conversation with Dirk Myers. "It occurred to me, when you were relating Herbert's very logical objection to searching for an actor who had been the fake doctor, how much likelier it would be for a woman to have learned how to take blood. All sorts of women do it as medical assistants: any woman who'd been a lab technician, you know, the sort who come around to your room in the hospital and keep taking blood for what I've always been certain is the doctors' own research; then there are the women at blood donor centers; nurses; somehow it seemed more logical that it might have been a woman who'd learned to draw blood, and then gone on to something else. I asked Dr. Myers if he was certain Patrice had mentioned a man. He wasn't, though I think he thinks he'd have noticed if she had used a female pronoun. Doesn't get us much further, does it?''

"I can't see that it gets us anywhere at all. Perhaps it widens the field a little. Just what we needed."

"Archer, poor dear; hasn't the biography got any further up here? Has it all been frustration and waste?"

"Not entirely. But we're so bogged down in her death, we can't seem to manage to think about her life. And there is something about this place that makes one want to cash in one's chips. I mean, two more weeks, and *I* might walk into the lake, and I've never before considered suicide for a minute."

"Why don't you go back to New York? You could even catch the last shuttle tonight." Kate looked at her watch. "Well, it would be a close call, but they start early in the morning."

"Are you coming?"

"I don't know, Archer. I had certainly planned to. But I wonder if I mightn't stay and work out one or two things."

"I should think you'd work them out better at home with Reed."

"You may be right. I'm going to call him now. I think I'll call from here, and not risk the phone in the president's house. It's not that I have a suspicious nature, it's just that I'd be wondering at every click."

Archer was almost out of the room when Kate called him back. "Sorry," she said. "Let me get all this straight. When Patrice died, her children came up here and removed, as far as they knew, all her manuscripts and papers. They didn't bother with her business file

161

until it was delivered to Sarah a long time later. All the papers went to the Berg Collection. Why not to the Clare library, by the way, or the Sophia Smith collection at Smith College?''

''I wondered that too. Sarah is a New Yorker, and had met Lola Szladits, that marvelous woman who runs the Berg Collection. It seemed to Sarah, once the Berg agreed to accept the papers, the obvious thing to do. Since Patrice had, as it then appeared, killed herself at Clare, that hardly bespoke her vast affection for the place. Anyway, her will stated clearly that the children were to do what they wanted, and so they did, not that George had any violent feelings in the matter.''

''We have ignored George, Archer. You don't think he might have been having a psychotic episode and done in Mama? I mean, we really do have to think of everything.''

''Herbert and I have thought of all this, believe it or not, and even went so far as to check what I suppose would have to be called alibis. George, at the operative time, was at a geologist's conference, or convention, or whatever geologists have, and was within sight of several hundred people constantly, as well as being three thousand miles away. Sarah, we determined, could, physically, have done it, whatever ''it'' is—that is, she wasn't unequivocally somewhere else with lots of disinterested witnesses; but I don't believe it for a minute, and neither do you. Everyone around here was milling about, and no one at Clare College had what could possibly be called an alibi. It was just like *Gaudy Night,* if you really want to know.''

''Veronica is certainly a likely subject, speaking of detective novels. I mean, her emotions toward Patrice were so strong and so conflicted, it's easy enough to imagine her killing a woman she had, after all, sued. But then, why keep insisting that it was murder when everyone was still happy to consider it suicide?''

"Why sue someone and then ask for forgiveness and befriend them again?"

"Archer! Do you think it's Veronica?"

"At this moment I'm prepared to think it's Dr. Myers. After all, the only evidence we have for his whole story is him."

"Patrice didn't write in her journal about the pancreas bit?"

"No. Not a word. But then, it wouldn't be like her to write that. She didn't write about the breast cancer, either, till long after it was over. I think she only wrote about things she was able to get under some kind of control by writing them down. The real anxieties were left to float, at least until they'd settled a bit. I'm pretty sure of that."

"No doubt you're right. But if the damn woman had arranged her own murder, she couldn't have cooperated better. There's not a shred of evidence anywhere, of anything."

"What else is new? Sorry Kate, but I think I'll retire and set my alarm for sunrise. New York and Herbert, here I come. And don't worry yourself into a frenzy. We must, I keep telling Herbert, return to the happy abandon of our Chinese restaurant meeting. Anyway, we must get on with the biography, and stop trying to decide on how Dickens would have ended *Edwin Drood*. It seems to me a similar problem."

Having bid Archer goodbye and gained permission from Lucy and Bertie to telephone from their bedroom, Kate went upstairs and called Reed.

"Ah," he said. "What plane are you taking? I've got in a good supply of all the appropriate materials of celebration. How's that for a try at the new polysyllabic mode, Kate? Are you there? Are you all right?"

"Reed. Could you find me a man? Or a strong, vigorous woman prepared for hard labor? Over the weekend."

163

"I take it I will not do, or you might have mentioned it."

"It has to be someone whose word is indisputable; no interest in this case, no connection to anyone in it. Also, I have to tell you, this person and I will probably end up in court, charged with assault, battery, and whatever all the other things are."

"Kate, you are not preparing to attack someone! Or to hold them up with a gun? My darling, please listen. . . ."

"Of course not. But I may break and enter, more or less. Yes, that describes it rather well. Reed, please don't worry. Can you find me someone?"

"How about a police officer off duty, or a detective from the force?"

"Well, considering that what I have in mind is a teensy bit illegal, maybe it better be a retired detective or policeman; but not too long retired. I really mean it when I say hard work."

"Oh, God. And if I don't find you someone, you'll find someone yourself who will certainly be worse. All right, give me a while. Where can I call you back?"

"Here, within an hour. If you can't find anyone in that time, I'll call you later. I have to think."

"Give me the number. How I hate it when you think. Promise you have no weapon of any sort in mind. Remember, I'm about to become a professor of criminal procedure."

Kate gave him the number and rang off. Downstairs, she accepted a brandy from Lucy and asked a few questions about the college. As she had thought, that kept them going happily for far longer than it took Reed to ring back. He had a man for her and the number at which to reach him.

"Please don't worry," Kate assured him. "I may even change my mind. It's not a bit dangerous, except for the possibility of being sued."

"Well," Reed said, "that's reassuring. With your

permission, I shall engage counsel now. Any particular law firm you prefer?''

The next evening, at seven-thirty, in front of the closed administration building, Kate met the man Reed had found for her, whose name was O'Malley, and who asked to be called Bob. Though insisting on being called Bob, he called her Mrs. Amhearst, and Kate decided not to argue with him. She had enough on her mind. It was clear that this was some old acquaintance of Reed's who had agreed to this caper as a favor to him. If that favor consisted of allowing and even helping his wife to act like a fool, that was Amhearst's business. But Kate was Mrs. Amhearst in his eyes; had she been anything else, he wouldn't be here.

''Waiting for the dark, are we?'' he said. ''Going to dig, are we?'' He pointed to the shovels and pickax Kate had lugged with her.

''Yes. To both questions. What a long time it takes to get dark. Thank heaven it's an undistinguished evening; the sun has gone down without making a fuss about it.'' This last was a direct quote from Sylvia Townsend Warner, whose letters were still whirling around in Kate's mind when Patrice's affairs could be persuaded to subside, but she saw no point in mentioning the fact to Bob O'Malley. He didn't look the sort of man to care for quotations, or even tolerate them.

''We got to carry these shovels far?''

''Quite far. Is one too heavy for you? I'll carry one and the pickax.'' Kate was beginning to wonder if he belonged to a municipal union.

''I can carry it. But why not drive to close to where we're going?''

''I haven't got a car. Do you have one?''

''Yeah. I thought you'd have a car.''

''I think it would be better to go by the campus paths. Less noticeable than driving around here at night. Ready?'' Kate looked at him sternly. She had somehow imagined someone a little more cooperative. Still, he would be wonderful on the witness stand, she consoled herself.

It took them fifteen minutes to reach their destination, but it seemed longer. Bob's mood had not improved. "Digging is one thing; carrying another," he said, which convinced Kate he did belong to a municipal union.

"Well," she said. "Now we're digging."

Bob looked up at the darkened house. "How do we know they won't come back and find us at it?"

"Because I've given them tickets to a gala concert of the Boston Symphony Orchestra."

"That's what house thieves always do," Bob said darkly. "Send people theater tickets and then clean the place out while they're gone."

"I didn't claim originality for the idea," Kate said. "Only efficiency. We dig here."

"Good thing you brought that pickax; ground's still frozen. Now, what is it we're supposed to be looking for?"

Kate told him.

Chapter 15

Oh yes, between 50 and 60 I think I shall write out some
very singular books, if I live.
                                    VIRGINIA WOOLF

*7*he following week was anguish, in varying degrees, for everyone. President Norton, wrestling with
the recommendations of the task force and Kate's by-
now-heated investigations into the Patrice affair, found
only one thing to be grateful for: the college was on vacation; no students remained to observe the untoward
happenings, chief of which was the arrival of the police,
preceded by several plainclothes detectives, to make an
arrest. Whether they were about to press charges of
murder, or, as they insisted, merely ask questions in
connection with their investigations, was a distinction
in which the president found little comfort.

Archer and Kate at their urban universities went
back to teaching, though how entirely their minds were
devoted to their pedagogical pursuits was probably not
worth inquiring. Herbert, nonetheless, asked. "I
find," Kate said, "that while I'm actually in the room
teaching, I can't think of another thing. Ardent bridge
players have told me that is also true of bridge. Perhaps

it's true of anything to which one gives one's whole attention. But before and after my thoughts are entirely with you, Herbert.''

For it was, of course, Herbert who had to undertake all the work of investigation, now that his vacation had started. He flew back and forth between New York and Boston, and once even to St. Louis, hiring cars, at Kate's expense and with what seemed to him total abandon, to convey him between airports and his various destinations.

Kate and Archer cheered him on, in person when he arrived, panting from his latest foray, on the telephone as he reported in from what he was beginning to call the field. ''You want to get to the bottom of this, you know you do,'' Kate said. ''Then you and Archer can get back to the biography with a clear mind.''

''I shall never have a clear mind again,'' Herbert moaned. ''Why can't we leave it all to the police?; they will act, Reed promises, in the fullness of time.''

''Look at it this way,'' Kate said. Archer tended, guiltily, to agree with Herbert about leaving things to the slow and uncertain machinations of the police. ''When you come to write up the startling end of Patrice's life, you want to be able to say you were there, you personally investigated, you personally can testify. So much more persuasive than the assumptions and guesswork of most biographies.''

''There is that,'' Herbert said, off to the airport.

Reed was alternately helpful and clucking, Kate felt, as though he'd been a professor of criminal procedure for years. ''Many's the time you leapt into cars and been off to a homicide, at least in your youth,'' Kate said. ''Or so you told me; before you became the great litigator, of course.''

Reed groaned, and tried to smooth the way of the investigators as best he could. In this, as in any profession, connections and networks shorten labors remarkably.

"And of course," Reed remarked from time to time, "you shall be up on charges of breaking and entering."

"I did not break and enter," Kate said. "I only entered, through a bathroom window I opened from the top. And if I'd weighed a pound more, I'd never have made it. I didn't take a thing. I just looked around a little." Reed groaned. "If you must know," Kate said, momentarily closing the discussion, "I was glad of a little activity. I'd just been complaining to Madeline how I did nothing but talk, talk, talk."

"O'Malley said, for a woman, you talked very little. I should have known that was an ominous sign. Have you noticed, by the way, the peculiar affinity you have developed for crime in Massachusetts?"

"Not a bit peculiar; that's where most of the colleges are. There're five in a consortium near Northampton and Amherst where I've never even been."

"I wonder," Reed said, "if they know how lucky they are."

In the end Kate went back to Clare College to explain it all to the president. The poor woman, as Kate was coming to think of her, had cleared an hour of her schedule which was far from easy. Kate apologized.

"It's not your fault," the president said. "I'm grateful to you for what you've done. At least, I think I am. The only trouble with rearranging one's schedule is that it's always the pleasant things that have to go. One can put off a colleague, but not a trustee, or an outraged donor. Shall we start at the beginning? I mean, the beginning of your stay here?"

"There's little point in that," Kate said. "All I did was bumble around and talk to people and ask foolish questions. We, Archer and I, had a little luck, but not much. And yet, if I hadn't come, the truth is, I think they'd have got away with it. It was a very clever little scheme."

"The Geddes."

"Yes. Both of them, I think. But that will be for their

169

lawyers to straighten out. I think it was what the psychologists call a *folie à deux*. But I've often thought that was a not bad description of most marriages: a blending of neuroses. Sorry. I do tend to wander, but I've never reported to a college president before. I'll try to keep on track.''

President Norton did not smile. She waited. Then she said: "You might begin with the Friday episode of digging up the Geddes lawn. What made you suspect them in the first place?''

"Oddly enough, I didn't; not in the first place. I suspected a lot of other people more: Veronica, several members of the faculty from various departments, a doctor. I even persuaded myself, almost, that Patrice might have decided to do the amazing thing of drowning herself in the lake in the middle of the night, leaving an almost wholly inappropriate, but apparently quite suitable, suicide note. Somewhere during my week here, I became convinced she had been murdered. One of the things that convinced me was that someone had tried before, though in a very indirect and chancy way. That's one of the bits of evidence poor Herbert has been rustling up.''

"You have lost me,'' the president said. "What attempt? And who is Herbert?''

"Sorry. Herbert is the other biographer, with Archer. He had a vacation when we all had to go back to work. The other attempt was an impersonation of a doctor, to convince Patrice that she had a fatal, close-to-terminal cancer. It was a clever try, and knowing Patrice's views on death, it might have worked. I'm fairly sure the suicide note was written then, by her murderers.''

"The one we found, mentioning Charlotte Perkins Gilman.''

"Yes. That was clever. It referred to a woman she admired, referred to cancer, if anyone really looked into it, and saved them from having to try to imitate Patrice's style at length, always risky. I suspect that

170

they planned to help along any plans she may have had for suicide after the cancer scare, but I can never prove that, or guess how. The whole episode was extremely ironic all the same, and a great lesson in causation, or the lack thereof. As it turned out, Patrice had had cancer, of the breast. But no one but her children and, later, her doctor, knew that. Her murderers were counting on her belief in death if life was not worth living; they didn't know all they had going for them, or how likely their threat of a new cancer would seem to her."

"I never knew," the president said. "I wish I had. I mean, that she had had breast cancer."

"I did a lot of my usual sort of guesswork," Kate went on. "I have a habit of being inspired by literature. Archer said that the end of this case would be as impossible to solve as the end of *Edwin Drood*. A novel Dickens wrote twenty-three chapters of and never lived to finish. Figuring out what he meant to do is one of the more popular literary games, like writing sequels to *Pride and Prejudice*."

"I seem," the president said, "to have lost my way somewhere around your mention of Dickens."

"Sorry. The point about *Edwin Drood* is that there's a character in it, named Datchery, who is clearly in disguise, though who he really is and what he looks like we will never know. There are also twins, boy and girl, and the girl is clearly going to impersonate. . . ." The president was beginning to look as though she had been trapped in the room with a wealthy alumna who turned out to be, not only an escaped lunatic, but impoverished.

"I'll try and spare you my train of thought," Kate hastened to say. "Anyway, I thought of disguise, and the oddities of gender, which we had also been discussing in your task force, and . . ." Kate paused. "I came to realize that the whole problem, when you came right down to it, was how she was found drowned in the lake, no bruises, no drugs, and it was still murder. How do you get a fairly good-sized and vigorous woman to the center of a largish lake? If she'd been drugged or knocked unconscious the autopsy would have shown it. That, when all was said and done, was the problem."

The president nodded, looking somewhat relieved; they were back with facts. "And then," Kate said, "it all hit me at once, like a thunder clap. The new lawn you mentioned. The swimming pool. His longitudinal study. I took a walk and decided to dig, or maybe I decided to dig after Archer mentioned Dickens. Anyway, if we couldn't find any evidence, we'd all be uncertain forever. I figured, if I was wrong, I would apologize, pay up, pretend to have been drunk, cavorting with Mr. O'Malley for ridiculous reasons of my own, whatever. But, as you know, I wasn't wrong."

"You found a pipe. That much I have gathered."

"Yes. It led from the lake to his pool, and enabled him to fill the pool with lake water. He had to redo the lawn to cover the digging. And the pipe, of course. Somehow, he drowned Patrice in the pool. He had to be sure, you see, that lake water would be found in her lungs. The ordinary chlorinated water wouldn't have done at all. It's easier, of course, to drown someone in a pool than to get them into a lake where they would struggle, you might be seen, etcetera. The medical examiner, or whatever he's called in Massachusetts, says she was drowned, clearly. I'll spare you the medical details of drowning. They—there were probably two of them—held her underwater in the pool, being careful not to bruise her. Perhaps they got her drunk, though there was very little liquor in her body. There was some, anyway. I'm fond of the sodium pentothal theory, but there are problems with that. In the course of all this investigation, I learned a lot about swimming pools. The Geddes pool was concrete, and therefore had to be emptied each year and refilled in June to keep it from cracking in the winter. There are also plastic pools which keep their water from one year to the other, but that is hardly germane."

"Hardly. What did you break into the house to look for?"

"Oh dear, you must really try to forget that. I was looking for two things. Actually, I was only looking for one, a manuscript of the book Patrice had been writing, which I didn't exactly find, I'll come back to that in a minute—have you ever noticed how difficult it is to tell a story in order?"

"I have noticed," the president said, just not adding, Kate felt, the word lately.

"While I was in the house," Kate said, rewarding this almost-sally with a smile, "Bob O'Malley said, 'Why don't we look for the pump?' 'Pump?' said I 'He had to pump the water up,' O'Malley said; 'it didn't climb up through the pipe of its own free will. Water doesn't, you know,' We found a sump pump in the basement, and O'Malley thought that might have done very well. You did ask me," Kate added. She badly wanted a cigarette, but felt the president had enough to bear.

"The rest of the week, we've been checking on things. That Gladys Geddes had trained as a nurse, long ago. I even got myself up with a wig and glasses and sandles, and walked into my department at the university, and no one recognized me. That part was rather fun; it's easier if you're older, so that people don't really look at you, as they don't in our society. Then, of course, we had to establish what was going on here on the day Patrice died. There were reunions, graduation the next day, all of that. We located (with your kind permission) an alumna who had talked to Patrice at six that evening. We could find no one who saw her afterward. She had refused to attend one of the class dinners, pleading tiredness and the need for an early night. How the Geddes got her there—oh, just stop in for a drink of your favorite Laphroaig—perhaps, we shall never know. At dinnertime there was no one around. No one would have any reason to be near the Geddes house anyway. They drowned her, stashed the body in the house, and later that night, dragged it, or took it in a boat to the middle of the lake, putting rocks in the pockets. Or they may have done that earlier. They left the note in her apartment—no problem getting in, they must have got themselves a key made. This had been in the works a long time."

"But why?"

"You don't have to prove motive for a crime; Reed has always told me that. But I can guess. For one thing, they hated her; simply hated her. No, I know that will never do in court, particularly since Professor Geddes had been careful to speak of her with affection, and Gladys made her detestation general enough to include all women professors. Herbert, poor dear, when he's been on planes, has been reading the first volume of Geddes's longitudinal study. There're still a lot of facts to be gathered, but I think he was in trouble; funds have been shrinking for research generally, and especially in the social sciences. (The humanities, of course, have never had enough to notice anyway.) A lot of his students had moved over to work with Patrice who was, you see, on his turf. She had developed whole new theories of middle age. We know only a few of them from her journal. She began to see that many women's lives particularly were lived by another pattern: beginning again just when it was all supposed to be over. A life wholly apart from youthful sexual attractions and domestic services. The group Geddes was studying allowed him to suggest that late middle age for women was a very down time, and here was Patrice, already famous and likely to be listened to, writing what might even have been a sort of *Passages* of late middle age, though I doubt it. Patrice was nothing of a journalist. I'm not sure whether he intended to destroy her work or steal it. Even if he tells us, that will not necessarily be the truth. He may not know himself. What we know now is that he destroyed her manuscript, or did not find it. But he kept her disks."

"Her disks?"

"Yes. Patrice wrote on a word processor. Of course, that was one of those things the daughter never got around to mentioning; why should she? They sold it with the other things, since neither child wanted it. Sarah had found no disks anywhere. That seemed odd, to say the least, but she assumed her mother had destroyed them before killing herself. I don't suppose you keep a bottle of Laphroaig in your office, in a secret place?"

"A bottle of what?" the president said, looking fearful. Kate decided she had stayed long enough.

"Nice to have met you," she said, rising to her feet, and shaking the president's hand. "I'll be looking forward to the results of the task force."

"And," she said to Lucy and Bertie, collapsing on their couch, "I really think I behaved very well, all things considered."

"What you need," Bertie said, "is a drink. Now tell *us* all about it." Kate lay down and howled.

A week later still, all vacations over, they were back—Archer, Herbert, Kate, and, this time, Reed —in the Chinese restaurant where Kate and the biographers had first met.

"What you must do," Kate said to them, "is begin now where you left off. All obvious problems solved; all you have to do is to write the biography."

"Which will be given even more attention once Patrice's work on middle age is published," Reed said. "I'm here to testify that she was a genius about middle age. Perhaps she was also a genius about death. At least we know, whatever she might have done at seventy, she didn't do it at fifty-eight."

"She couldn't have," Kate said. "Not with her feelings about the book she was writing, rendered in her journal through Virginia Woolf's words. I guess, somewhere in the back of my mind, I always knew that."

"There is a teeny part of me," Archer said, "which wants to blame Sarah. I mean, my dear, if she'd only

175

looked through Mama's things, as any proper daughter ought to have done. We'd have known about the last part of the journal sooner, and we would have had those disks with the new book on it.''

"Unfair," Kate said. "I think Sarah would have looked in time; in fact, she had begun to. Because we love Patrice doesn't mean that she was the easiest mother to have had. I think Sarah was letting time pass, always a wise move when one can only cause catastrophes by rushing about and *doing* things. And she does have a busy life, you know. A profession, a husband, a baby.''

"In certain ways," Herbert said, "young women today are amazing. All I have is a job and a biography, and I'm swamped."

"There you are, you see," Kate said. "No time to look in files for disks. Disks are very thin, in their discreet little envelopes, and can be slipped into files among papers: I've learned that much.''

"But why?" Reed asked.

"Sarah would say Patrice was secretive: her generation. I understand. And just as well she was. Geddes found the manuscript *and* the first set of disks. Blessings to Patrice for having filed the back-up disks away.''

"It's odd, though," Reed said. "She was secretive about the book which I can well understand. I'm not inclined to talk about important things myself, never mind extended acts of creation. But given that, how did Geddes hear of it?''

"I've thought of that," Kate said. "But one does discuss scholarly matters with informed colleagues. Life cycles were Geddes's specialty. It was natural to choose him to talk to about it. Whether she actually told him about the book, or whether he guessed, we may never know.''

"But imagine," Archer said, "a whole book on three disks.''

"Eight-inch disks," Kate said, with a knowing air.

"You can get almost five hundred pages on that; maybe more."

"One gathers," Reed said, "that you have been doing research on word processing. Are we to become the proud owners of one, or is this all in the holy name of investigation?"

Kate grinned at him. She felt fine. Reed was over his crisis, which she knew to be deeper than his casual first mention of it might have indicated. And they had Patrice back. The new book, unfinished of course, was a bonus, but not the main thing, Kate thought. The main thing was Patrice herself, intact, as she was, or as close as they, or anyone, could come to what she was.

"I think about Veronica," Archer said. "How in the end she had nothing on to do with it. Yet I would have bet on her as involved, at least somehow."

"She was, I think," Kate said. "Looking back to the first time she and I met, I see that she was nervous, frightened, challenging me to suspect her. And then, she insisted that the murderer was a woman, though whether she believed that, or was throwing out another challenge, I'll never know. But her suit was important, after all. It probably suggested something to Geddes. If he stole Patrice's work, and if, after her death, anyone claimed it was hers, it would begin to look very suspicious that *two* people claimed they had been ripped off by Patrice. It would appeal to the there's-no-smoke-without-fire crowd, not to mention those happy to think any ill of her."

"I can't help wishing we had found another novel, too," Herbert said.

"We lost a great deal by her murder," Kate said. "In the thirteen years we may assume she would have allowed herself, who knew what she might have done? As I told Archer to his dismay, Sylvia Townsend Warner wrote her biography of T. H. White at seventy, and some people consider that the best biography ever written. Sylvia Townsend Warner had never met her subject either," Kate said to Herbert. She felt that Herbert needed cheering on, after all his investigative efforts. Besides, he was the sort of professor who worked with documents and recorded facts: murder had never been envisioned by him, let alone as the subject of his work.

"You solemnly promised," Archer said, "never to mention Sylvia Townsend Whatsis again. She reminds me of Clare College. Beastly unfair of me, since she was never there, but who is to escape from the associations life bestows?"

"In fact," Reed said, "though I have to admit you all, particularly Kate, gave me one or two bad moments, I think you should be very proud of yourselves. My only worry," he said, as the food arrived and was elegantly parceled out by the head waiter, "is that you will all spend too long basking in the glory of your achievement."

"Not a chance," Kate told him. "As Lytton Strachey said, 'Success came to us too late to make us hop on our perches.' "

"Where did he say that?" Herbert asked.

"To Virginia Woolf, of course," Kate said.

"I prefer Martin Buber," Herbert answered. " 'We must relinquish undirected plenitude in favor of the one taut string, the one stretched beam of direction.' "

"Eat your lemon chicken, Herbert," Archer said.

About the Author

Amanda Cross is the pseudonym of a New York City university professor. This is the seventh Amanda Cross mystery, following IN THE LAST ANALYSIS, THE JAMES JOYCE MURDER, POETIC JUSTICE, THE THEBAN MYSTERIES, THE QUESTION OF MAX, and DEATH IN A TENURED POSITION.

Attention Mystery and Suspense Fans

Do you want to complete your collection of mystery and suspense stories by some of your favorite authors? Raymond Chandler, Erle Stanley Gardner, Ed McBain, Cornell Woolrich, among many others, and included in Ballantine's new Mystery Brochure.

For your FREE Mystery Brochure, fill in the coupon below and mail it to: